The Ghost Wore Polyester

A novel by
Gail Koger & S.J. Smith

CrossTIME
an imprint of the Crossquarter Publishing Group
PO Box 8756
Santa Fe, NM 87504-8756

Although the murder of journalist Don Bolles really happened, the following is a work of fiction. Any resemblance to actual persons, living or dead, is purely coincidental.

Library of Congress Cataloging-in-Publication Data

Koger, Gail, 1950-
The ghost wore polyester : a novel / by Gail Koger & S. J. Smith.
    p. cm.
  ISBN 1-890109-76-2 (pbk.)
  1. Women in the book industries and trade—Fiction. 2. Journalists—Crimes against—Fiction. 3. Booksellers and bookselling—Fiction. 4. New Age movement—Fiction. 5. Sedona (Ariz.)—Fiction.
  I. Smith, S. J. (Sally Jayne), 1948- II. Title.
  PS3611.03655G48 2004
  813'.6—dc22
                        2004006967

(continued from previous page)

Acknowledgements

The Authors wish to extend our thanks all the way to the other side to Jan Ross for sharing her insight, her foresight, and her second sight.

We also wish to acknowledge the excellent coverage over the years of the Don Bolles murder by the *Arizona Republic*.

The brutal car bomb murder of reporter Don Bolles dominated Arizona headlines in the summer of 1976. Even after all the trials, re-trials, convictions and overturnings, no one really knows exactly why he was killed. To this day many are convinced that those convicted were set up, that the real killer or killers were never caught, that conspiracies to conceal the facts are still at work. The truth may never be known. The murder and subsequent Arizona Project of the Independent Reporters and Editors are matters of history – what follows is a work of complete fiction. Names, places, and incidents either are a product of the authors' imaginations or are used fictitiously. With that in mind, hang on and enjoy the ride.

—*Sally & Gail*

Dedication

This first one is stretched pretty thin, but the sentiments remain undiluted. It's for my family – Dale, Carrie, Brian – without whose fierce love, loyalty and support I couldn't be me. And of course, always for *chocolate*.

Sally

This book is dedicated to my parents for their unswerving support and to Dorothy and Darcie for always being there for me.

Gail

Prologue

I'd taken the wrong turn. Again. Story of my friggin' life — eh?

Earlier in the day, I'd stopped for gas and a quick bite in the town of Holbrook, Arizona. It barely qualifies as a town — one of those places by-passed by both the interstate and prosperity. A quart of chocolate milk and a package of Hostess Ding Dongs from a convenience store was dinner. In the midst of my chocolate feeding frenzy, I missed the sign to get back on I-40 — just blew right by it. So, there I was, sitting in my new blue four wheel drive Toyota 4Runner, watching the sun set on the Painted Desert. It was breathtaking. A barren landscape awash in watercolor hues of lavender, rose and turquoise. The sun set it on fire in a crimson glow.

Sometimes there's a lot to be said for taking the wrong turn. The road less traveled and all. Did I say "less traveled?" Try deserted. Not a single soul in sight. The low whistle of the desert wind was the only sound. Wait a minute. It was dead calm — there *was* no desert wind. Oh, shit. I got out of the car and watched the left rear tire go down with the setting sun.

"No problem. I'll just call Triple A," I said to the desert. But when I flipped open my cell phone, "Yes problem. No signal. What now?" Sound like a pitch for "On-Star" or what?

Fighting down panic, I pulled myself up by my Nike straps. "You can do this, Tildy."

The owner's manual gave step-by-step instructions and I have to say, it wasn't going too bad until...

"Insert the lug wrench over the nut and turn counterclockwise." Sounds simple enough, you say. That's what I thought too.

The penlight clenched between my teeth, I angled it down on the lug nut in question. The head of the wrench fit like a dream — like they were made for each other. Imagine that. I was feeling pretty handy, just call me Tildy the Tool-Time Gal, when I noticed it wasn't moving. I leaned harder. Hmm. Harder. Nope. Pounding — kicking — until finally, I was jumping up and down on the blasted thing. Thank God it finally gave way. Only four more to go. A sob of self-pity choked me, but I refused to give in to it, and moved the wrench to the next lug nut.

* * * * *

Two sweaty, grimy hours later — I was sitting in the dirt, leaning back against the car, black crap all over my face and hands, not to mention my winter white virgin wool slacks. But lo and behold, the spare was on the left rear wheel. The tire with the hole was in the back of the car. I was queen of all I surveyed, feeling pretty good about myself. Tildy, Warrior Princess.

When off in the distance, something wild howled. And then something else yipped. And the Warrior Princess suddenly realized she was all by herself in the middle of the desert with the snakes and the scorpions and the "what-evers" making all the racket.

I jumped up, threw the rest of the tire stuff in the back. The howling was definitely closer. And when the howling gets close, the scared get going.

I opened the door and put one foot up on the running board when something very cold and very wet touched — no, slimed — my ankle.

"Yeeek!!" I jumped into the car, jerked my feet up and grabbed for the door handle just as a furry blur landed smack in my lap — "Ohmigod!" — then it started to whine.

When I could see again, I found myself looking down into the small brown, terrified eyes of a matted dirty little West Highland Terrier.

The howling was closer by the second and that sent the little guy into a fresh round of shivering.

"Where'd you come from, fella?"

I slammed the door, muffling the cries of the prowling predators. He put his paws on my chest and began to lick my face — I could almost hear him: "Thank you. Thank you. Thank you."

As I held him close against me, something opened up inside, and I began to cry. He gave me some more kisses and my sobs turned to laughter.

There we were, both abandoned, both strays. Two lost souls who somehow managed to find each other in the middle of nowhere. We belonged to each other — belonging is good. I gave him a name right there on the spot — Haggis. Love at first sight.

Yep. Sometimes there's a lot to be said for taking the wrong turn...

Chapter One

...but not always.

The first wrong turn was twenty years ago when I stood at the altar with Andrew the Anus and said "I do," when I really didn't. It's taken me all this time to find the right path.

My name is Matilda MacNamara — my friends call me Tildy.

I see things, sometimes. And sometimes I just know things. Back when I was a kid, Mom passed it off as a vivid imagination. The neighborhood mothers decided I was a disruptive influence. The nuns told everyone I was Satan's spawn and threw holy water on me. That was a fun one. But when I was fifteen I found out what all the hunches, all the visions really were — I'm psychic (that's *psychic*, folks, not *psycho*). My Grandma told me. I was pretty surprised to hear from her since she'd been dead for two years.

To Andrew the Anus, my "loving" husband, it was an embarrassing nuisance. What full-of-himself big-time Chicago lawyer needs a carnival side-show freak for a wife? To say he had no real use for me is putting it mildly.

The straw that broke Andrew's back landed during our Christmas dinner party when two martinis got the best of me and I blurted out to the senator's wife, "Oh my God, Bunny! Your gardener gave you herpes!?"

The senator choked on a bite of lobster and turned purple. We called 911. When the paramedics wheeled out the senator, it was pretty obvious the party was over and so was my marriage.

Andrew closed the door behind the last guest. "I'm done with you." He strode purposefully into the bedroom. "I hate that goddamn soothsayer bullshit."

I trailed behind him miserably. "Okay, I could have been more discreet. I don't know what came over me."

"The same thing that always comes over you. Stupidity." He pulled a suitcase off the closet shelf and began loading up his designer boxers.

He was serious, leaving for good this time.

"Andrew, please don't go." Yeah, I was groveling — and I'm not even sure why. You couldn't call it a marriage, not really. But that didn't stop me from being scared.

And suddenly — WHAM! There's this vision of Andrew and Elizabeth Worthington, his bleached blonde law partner with the saline implants doing the nasty in her antique Victorian bed. It was vivid, in full Technicolor with Surround Sound, yet. Andrew hadn't touched me in three months — not that I minded — and in all honesty, he never touched me like he "touched" Elizabeth Worthington.

I stood there, my mouth hanging open like a bass, tears of humiliation streaming down my cheeks.

"You're doing it with Elizabeth!?"

He sneered, "Figure that out on your own, did you? Some psychic you are," and walked out.

I escaped onto the balcony and stood looking out over Lake Michigan. The December air was cold and sharp, like a slap in the face — yet, the velvet silence cocooned me comfortingly.

It was easy to rationalize staying with him all those years. I'd chosen the devil I knew over the devil I didn't.

But standing there watching a freighter head out to open sea, its lights flickering on the horizon, I realized maybe those weren't my only choices.

The front door slammed. The sound of finality. It hit me like a blow to the gut. For the first time in my life, I was alone. I went back inside, laid down on the bed and stayed there for forty-eight hours.

I was angry. I was scared. I was a complete wreck. Didn't comb my hair. Didn't brush my teeth. But I did eat chocolate — eat, hell — I binged! Chocolate candy. Chocolate cake. Chocolate brownies. Chocolate ice cream. Chocolate milk. Chocolate covered potato chips. You name it. I ate it. If chocolate was heroin, I'd be dead from an overdose.

On the third day, I got up and hired the best damn divorce attorney in Chicago. It turned out he was well worth the money. My "half" was one and three-quarters of a million dollars.

So there I was, footloose, fancy-free. Who was I kidding? I didn't have a clue what to do or where to go. One year and six weeks from the day Andrew left me, a letter from a Phoenix attorney found me still sitting in my living room doing nothing, killing time.

My great Aunt Matilda — the reason I got stuck with this swell name — had crossed over. She was always a bit of a weirdo, but I loved her. I guess I was the only one who did. She left everything to me including her home and book store in northern Arizona.

Sedona.

Red-rock country.

A place where psychics (and maybe even psychos) are not only accepted, but celebrated.

So I loaded up the car, took my hefty divorce settlement, my maiden name and hit the road.

* * * * *

I drove into Sedona, Arizona, exactly one week from the day I'd left Chicago. Just outside of town, just like everyone else, I had to pull off the road and stare. I got out of the car. Haggis jumped out too.

I had never seen anything like it. The cliffs, red as a persimmon, were dotted with clumps of jade cedar. Under a turquoise sky, Bell Rock glowed pink and cinnamon and scarlet.

The cathedral serenity of this wonderful place touched my soul. Psychic currents coursed through me like electricity.

The Vortex. They say Sedona is one of those spooky places. You know, paranormal stuff. Alien landings and psychic power points — like Stonehenge and Machu Pichu.

And I felt it. It took my breath. Healing tears filled my eyes and a sob of pure happiness burst from me. Haggis yipped and jumped up into my arms, licking away my tears. "You're right, boy. We are home."

I drove along Highway 89, excited to begin my new life, just like old Theodore Schnebly who...

Chapter Two

...back in 1901, packed up his life and his wife Sedona, and left Missouri, heading west — just like me. One year later, they settled in the gorgeous red-rock country of northern Arizona. A whole year. Geez. Guess they took a few wrong turns themselves.

Back then, Sedona wasn't much more than a small cattle settlement. Today, according to the brochure: "Sedona is a bustling, picturesque vacation hot spot. The natural beauty, the psychic phenomenon, its proximity to Phoenix and the Grand Canyon. Brilliant red rock formations tower over an assortment of shops, restaurants, B and B's, world class resorts, museums and art galleries. Well-heeled tourists move along the sidewalks, chattering in a multitude of languages, taking good advantage of the thousand-and-one photos ops."

The Spirit of the Vortex bookstore was just past the "Y" on Highway 89-A in uptown Sedona. I circled and circled wondering if it was always so hard to find a place to park. The old Tildy would have just kept driving around looking for a parking spot, but the new Tildy — ruthless, predatory — simply stole one. A mini-van pulled out and I whipped in ahead of the car already waiting. Andrew would have been proud.

The other driver flipped me the bird and bellowed, "Who taught you to drive, you stupid bitch?"

It seemed like a rhetorical question, so I ignored him, put the leash on Haggis and got out of the car.

It was only about ten o'clock, but the town was already swarming with tourists. Hot damn! Potential customers. I was so excited I could hardly keep from jumping up and down. But I couldn't do that. I was an entrepreneur now — no jumping allowed. Screw it.

I jumped.

I danced.

I squealed.

Haggis danced, too. Other pedestrians gave us a wide berth. My high spirits were doused by the "closed" sign.

"Bummer," I said to Haggis, then, "Hello."

Just next door was paradise: Death By Chocolate.

Maybe I haven't mentioned it; but I, Tildy MacNamara, am one of the walking cursed, driven by a hunger that rules my every waking thought, that pounds in my soul like a siren song — chocolate. I was drooling on the window.

"Morning." A tall pleasant-looking woman came out of the chocolate shop with a bottle of Windex in one hand and a paper towel in the other. Her silver hair and gray eyes stood out against her tanned skin. She was dressed in a rose colored Indian-style skirt-and-blouse and nu-buck moccasin boots. An ornately tooled concha belt circled her waist. The most wonderful heavy necklace of inlaid turquoise and silver lay against her chest. I couldn't help but notice it — this sturdy gal was so tall, her throat was at eye level.

"That's really beautiful."

She saw I was staring at the necklace. Her hand rose to touch it. "It was a gift. Navajo squash blossom."

I stepped aside while she cleaned the nose prints and drool off the window. "Sorry," I muttered.

"Happens all the time." She reached down to scratch Haggis behind the ear. "What's your poison?"

* * * * *

She served me decadent chocolate cake outside on a cute little brick patio behind the chocolate shoppe. A cheerful fire in a red clay chimenea took the chill off the brisk February air. A slight rustle carried the song of wind chimes over the otherwise quiet nook. From the store, I heard voices and the ring of the cash register.

The Windex lady stood by expectantly, so I dove head first into the chocolate cake. A tough job, but somebody had to do it.

One bite and I was hooked. "Oh my God. This should be against the law."

She smiled. "I know."

"What time do they open the bookstore?" I asked.

"It's kind of hit-and-miss over there since the owner died. Chloe does the best she can, but her clock's out of synch with the rest of the world. She's been holding the place together until the new owner gets here from back East."

I stuck out my hand. "She's here. I'm Tildy MacNamara, Matilda's niece."

She captured my hand within both of hers. "I'm Grace. Grace Mason."

Suddenly smoke stung my lungs and my eyes. Grace's touch burned; and when I looked down, her right hand was on fire. Hot flames licked out from under her shirt sleeve. I jerked away, but not fast enough to avoid the assault of a bellowing inferno and the agonized cries of someone caught within it.

"When was the fire?"

She frowned and looked down at the slash of white scar tissue across the back of her hand. "Oh, that. I tipped over a pan of hot fudge. Happened years ago. Been a lot more careful since."

"I bet."

Fudge, huh? So there you go. Once again, Andrew was proven right. Some psychic I am.

* * * * *

A half hour later, I opened the door to my very own bookstore and stepped inside. The smell of sweet incense and rich coffee filled my nostrils. The tinkle of wind chimes and strains of New Age music wafted throughout the place. Sunlight streamed through the windows, dancing magically off crystals scattered throughout the store. And books? Books everywhere. Books about astrology. Books about Tarot. Books about naturopathic healing. I ran my finger along the spines, loving everything about the place.

I loved the flagstones laid across the floor. I loved the rich earth tones and delicate patterns of the Turkish carpet which spaced off the reading nook. I loved the display cases full of intricately carved jewelry and talismans.

"Can I help you?"

I turned and found myself looking into the clearest blue eyes I'd ever seen. Clear, calm, and somehow familiar. And at total odds with the diamond nose stud, blue mascara, black lipstick and spiky lavender hair. The kids in Chicago looked like this a few years ago. I guess it takes a while for things to work their way west.

"I'm Tildy MacNamara," I stuck out my hand, "the new owner."

"Oh my gawd." She pulled me against her and hugged and hugged and hugged. "I can't believe you're here."

Haggis ran circles around us — yip, yip, yip.

I pulled back for a look at the whole package. She had on a neon green mohair sweater over orange leggings and purple calf high boots. I thought back to what Grace said about Chloe's clock being out of synch with the rest of the world. She never said anything about her being color blind, too.

"You must be Chloe."

"Oh, my gawd, you're psychic, too. We're going to be the best of friends." She smiled. "I just know it. You'll love it here. The store is awesome and wait 'til you see the house. It's so the bomb."

* * * * *

Chloe was right. It was the bomb — but not the way she meant it.

I found the old house on two acres of high-dollar creekside real estate, shaded by century-old apple trees. To get there, you head north out of town on Highway 89 about a mile and half, then turn where you see the stand of six mailboxes. The road dips down across the creek, over a rise and you're there. It's wonderful, quiet, the perfect hideaway.

My home (doesn't that sound nice?) is a two story piece of gingerbread with three bedrooms and one bath upstairs, and a converted bedroom and a bath downstairs. The kitchen was old, but tiled in a charming French blue-and-white pattern. The bathroom floors were done in the forties style with small black-and-white tiles. A porch with a veranda wrapped around the whole house, and there was a small New Orleans style balcony off the bedroom I'd claimed upstairs. A patch of yellowed grass and a flower garden gone to seed would need my attention come spring.

I have to admit I was a little intimidated. The place had charm but my work was definitely cut out for me. Everything needed updating. Sparks spit from the outlets whenever I turned on the microwave. Water wouldn't run through the ancient plumbing, but it did come through the Swiss-cheese roof.

So much to do. But by the time I finished, it would be well worth the effort.

After the first week, I figured out that running a psychic bookstore wasn't something you could just step into, so I promoted Chloe to store manager. Hell, she'd been running it for years, anyway — ever since Aunt Matilda got sick. I spent as much time there as possible, and I picked up more every day. I learned I'm a quick study and have a head for business. Eat your heart out, anal boy.

My personal life took longer, about four months or so. I needed time to familiarize myself with the town and its all too colorful inhabitants, and make Aunt Matilda's gentle old dowager of a Victorian mansion livable —

— all the while trying very hard to pretend the house wasn't haunted...

Chapter Three

At first I thought all the creaks and groans were just the complaints of an old house. But then, I began to sense a presence hanging around.

For instance, one night at three a.m., my bedroom TV suddenly blared to life. I erupted from a sound sleep to find John Travolta cavorting around a lighted dance floor in a satin shirt and tight pants.

"Jesus Christ." I reached for the remote and snapped it off.

Before my head even hit the pillow, John was back.

Click.

And back on.

I threw off the covers, got up and unplugged the friggin' thing. "Have to call that damn electrician back in the morning."

Haggis raised his head to see what was going on, then went right back to sleep — just like I hoped to do, when...

"Ah — ah — ah — ah. Stayin' alive. Stayin' alive."

Travolta was back. Now, don't get me wrong. I like the guy and all, but — **"Enough already!"**

And just like that. He was gone. I didn't hear from John or the Bee Gees for the rest of the night.

The next night I was pouring over my bookkeeping home study course, and having a swell time I might add, when the lights began to strobe like a disco show.

"Now what?"

The stereo kicked on with a rousing Donna Summer number. I would have blamed that on the electrician, too, except I don't have any Donna Summer CDs.

The next day, the doorbell rang constantly, every ten or fifteen minutes. Poor little Haggis got all excited every time and rushed over to see who was coming to visit. But when I opened the door, no one was ever there. Haggis growled and made a big deal out of sniffing the door mat.

The whole thing was making me crazy.

Then we got the cold spots. The first one was in the kitchen between the sink and the fridge. I walked through it a couple of times. It went away, or so I thought, until it popped back up in the bathroom. I was freezing my butt off every time I took a shower.

"Okay, pal," I said in my toughest voice to show whatever-it-was I meant business, "You wanna play hard ball? Batter up."

I consulted my local psychic guru and newly promoted store manager, Chloe, who recommended a cleansing.

Sounded like a plan. So, the next evening after we'd closed down the store, she came over wearing a hot pink caftan, beaded in fake gemstones, bearing all her "guru" paraphernalia: a tied bundle of sage, a bottle of holy water, a box of crystals, a few Feng Shui mirrors and — get this — a wreath of garlic cloves.

I stared at the garlic and gave her a look.

She just shrugged and drove a nail into the door to hang it on. "Can't hurt."

It was a scream to watch her. She set the sage on fire and while it smoked up the place like a clogged flue, she walked around the house chanting: "We seek to cleanse this home of negative energies."

She had to keep relighting the sage. I figured the "negative energies" didn't like the way it smelled and kept blowing it out. Can't say as I blamed them.

Chloe sprinkled the holy water around, then for good measure, she placed the crystals and Feng Shui mirrors at strategic spots.

When she was finished, Chloe stood back and had a good look around, breathed in deeply, then said dramatically, "This house is clean."

I flashed on the *Poltergeist* movie, and hoped this turned out better than that deal. Didn't that house disappear into some hell-hole at the end?

It didn't take long to figure out that as a psychic guru, Chloe sucked.

Not only was the cold spot still there, now it was following me around.

"Persistent bastard, aren't you? Why don't you just tell me what you want and get it over with?"

I went to bed that night wearing my socks because the cold spot was sitting on my feet. Dammit.

* * * * *

I am so friggin' scared I can't think straight. My car fishtails around the bend. The beams of my headlights careen wildly over the twisting roadway. Darkness surrounds me. Grasping skeletal fingers claw at the car, ripping shrieking metal away in strips. No, not fingers. Branches. Spiny branches whipping in the wind. The car starts to disintegrate around me. The cold night air blasts across my face. The tires squeal as I flee. Flee from what? I look in the rearview mirror to see -

Eyes. Glowing, malevolent eyes growing closer and closer. A demon swooping down to devour my very soul. No, not eyes. Not a demon. Lights. Headlights. A car, coming fast, coming too fast to escape.

And suddenly my car is gone and I'm rolling, tumbling over the asphalt. I get up and stumble, desperately trying to run. My legs won't move. I turn and the lights are everywhere, blinding me. Now it's too late and I cry out. Pain, such horrible pain. Blackness. At first there's nothing. No light. No sound. Nothing, then I hear —

— scraping. Metal against what? Stone? As my eyes focus I become aware of trees surrounding me. Dark menacing trees shrouded in a swirling mist, and something else. A dim shadow. Someone digging? Digging what?

And now, I'm dropping, falling down, down. A grave. Oh shit! A grave! Moist dirt is dumped on my face. In my mouth, in my eyes. I can't scream. I can't breathe.

I really can't breathe...

* * * * *

I sat straight up in bed, gasping for air.

"Jesus Christ! What the hell was that all about?" I was nearly in tears.

Haggis was whining.

"Sorry. I had to get your attention somehow," a male voice answered from the darkness.

I nearly jumped out of my skin. I did jump out of bed, grabbing for the Louisville Slugger beneath it.

There was a strange man in my room.

I swung the bat, but it went right through him, sending me spinning to land on my ass.

A ghost. About damn time he showed himself. "All right, Casper, let's have it."

"I need you to find out who murdered me."

I just sat and checked him out, resisting the urge to rub my aching ass.

He was a *Saturday Night Fever* Tony Manero evil twin: dark brown, poofed up hair; black rayon shirt open to the third button, curly chest hair peeking through; gold chains glittering at his throat; and his black pants were bellbottoms — polyester bellbottoms — tight, polyester bellbottoms — *really* tight polyester bellbottoms.

Haggis ran down to the foot of the bed and tried to lick his hand. It didn't work out all that well — ectoplasm being what it is. But it was a valiant slurp all the same.

Sprawling on the floor in front of a stranger, your panties showing, whether the stranger's alive or not, is a little undignified, so I hauled myself up and sat back down on the edge of the bed. "Let me get this straight. You want me to find out who murdered you? Is that all?" I asked.

"Yes." He had a smooth, sexy voice.

"Were you this dense when you were alive?"

He cocked his head and frowned. "What do you mean?"

"You were there at the time. Right?"

He nodded, still not getting it.

"Well," I continued slowly, as if I was talking to a three year old. "I'd think you'd already know who did it."

"Figures." He stood up and paced the room. Nice butt. "The first person who can see me after almost a quarter of a century is a smartass."

"Smartass? That does it." I slid my feet into my slippers and pulled my robe over my baggy tee-shirt which warns the world: *I've got a 44-caliber and a raging case of PMS.*

His next remark was drier than an Arizona riverbed in June. "Well, aren't we chic?"

"Better watch your step, buster." I pointed to my chest as I stood up and headed for the door. "I live by these words."

"Where are you going? If you're heading for the sage, save it for the turkey. It doesn't work," he smirked.

"So I see. I'm going to make some coffee. I've got a feeling this is going to be one hell of a story and I want to be wide awake to hear it." I turned back at the door. "You coming?"

* * * * *

He stared at the steaming coffee longingly. "I'd die for just one sip of that heavenly brew."

"Sorry, I would have offered you some, but...." I cocked one eyebrow at him over the rim of my cup. "Wait a minute. Did you just say die? Who's the smartass now?"

"Houston Powers." He stuck out his hand and we shook. Sort of. And it was kinda creepy.

"Tildy MacNamara."

"I know."

It suddenly came to me. "Oh shit. That was you in the shower."

"I didn't look," he said with a leer.

"Why don't I believe that?"

"Don't worry about it. I'm gay." He watched me. I think he wanted to see how I would react. "I said I'm gay."

I got up to pour another cup of coffee. "Like that makes it okay to be a Peeping Tom?"

Houston just shrugged. "Are you going to help me or not?"

"Dunno yet." I stirred Swiss mocha creamer into my coffee. "I can't believe you've been hanging around for almost twenty-five years. Didn't you see that movie? You should have gone into the light. What's wrong with you?"

"Too many loose ends." He gestured dramatically. "You can't imagine all the loose ends."

What a character. "Such as?"

"Well, for starters. Which one of the slimeballs I was investigating did me in?"

"Investigating?" This was starting to sound interesting.

"I'm an investigative reporter. I mean — was. I was an investigative reporter. You know, *the* Houston Powers."

I just stared at him.

He crossed his arms impatiently. "Houston Powers of *World News Magazine*?"

"Sorry. I've never heard of you."

This seemed to bother him a lot. He paced. And when I say paced, I mean paced. Right through the table, the wall and refrigerator, then he whirled. "You can't tell me you don't remember the case of Sasha? The guerilla terrorist who bombed the World News Magazine Building in 1970? I blew the lid off that story. It got me the Pulitzer. You know, Houston 'Ace Reporter' Powers?"

The expression on my face must have been as blank as my mind because he looked at me with suddenly forlorn eyes. "Has everyone forgotten me?" He began to pace again.

"Stand still. You're driving me crazy."

He did stop, but floated several inches off the floor, hands on his hips, foot tapping the air.

"It doesn't mean anyone has forgotten you. I don't remember because in 1970 I was in friggin' grade school and way too cool to be concerned with terrorists."

He plopped into the chair across from me. "Oh, well then."

"Wait a minute. Is that who murdered you?"

"Heavens no." He inhaled the coffee aroma. "God, that smells so good. Okay. Here's the scoop." He crossed his legs and leaned back. "Back in June of 1976, Don Bolles, a reporter for *The Arizona Republic*, was car-bombed, blown to smithereens. It took the poor bastard eleven days to die. He was working on a story about how the mob had their fingers stuck in nearly every aspect of Arizona business and politics. Land fraud. Dog racing. Election campaign pay offs. You name it. What Bolles learned cost him his life."

Houston told his story with passion.

"Okay," I said, "I'm hooked. Go on."

"The murder gave birth to the Arizona Project, galvanizing the IRE into a six month investigation of crime and corruption in the good ol' Grand Canyon State."

"IRE?"

"Investigative Reporters and Editors. Thirty-six journalists from around the country fanned out from their temporary headquarters in the Adams Hotel in Phoenix. It was a tribute to Bolles. A gesture to complete his work. I was one of those reporters."

"Oh my God! They killed you, too!? Who did it?"

"You don't listen very well, do you? That's what I need you to find out."

"Me! Like I know how to conduct a murder investigation? What did the police say?"

"How the hell am I supposed to know? I've been stuck here for twenty-five years. Your aunt didn't have a TV and she thought newspaper was just for lining the bird cage. Hell, for all I know, they may have gassed the guy already."

"Well if that's all you need, I can do that. The police report should be a matter of public record. Where were you when you were murdered?"

"Here."

"Great. I'll just go and get a copy and then you can be on your way. Piece of cake."

Right. Piece of cake, my fanny. It wasn't cake at all. It was...

Chapter Four

... cookies. Tough cookies. And I was about to come up against a few, like the very next day.

After leaving Chloe in charge of the bookstore, I headed over to the P.D. The store was busy as hell, but I didn't expect to be gone long. And this was important personal business. If I was ever going to get a decent night's sleep again, I had to send that disco wannabe packing.

It was a perfect summer day. High eighties. A light breeze stirred the trees. Driving along 89A I kept breaking out into song: *Stayin' alive. Stayin' alive.* Damn that guy.

From their perch on Roadrunner Drive the Sedona Police promise to protect and serve. Yep, all twenty of them. The terra cotta stucco building is the same Santa Fe style you find everywhere in Sedona with the same skimpy parking.

After cruising the lot for fifteen minutes, I finally pulled into a spot marked "Chief of Police." He wasn't using it and I was only going to be in there a minute or two. Famous last words. Right?

A strapping young police officer sat behind the counter. His leg was in a thigh-high cast and he had it propped up on a chair. Two wide-eyed blondes giggled adoringly as he regaled them with tales of Wild West daring do.

The young cop put up his dukes for emphasis. "There I was. Just me and those three drunk cowboys. Each one of 'em six-foot-four if he was an inch and built like a linebacker."

The blondes oohed and aahed.

"I squared off..."

I couldn't believe it. The jackass was literally swaggering. You've got to admire a guy who can pull that off in a chair with his leg in a cast.

"Excuse me, Officer?"

He glanced over and after dismissing my meager bustline and decidedly unprovocative outfit, "Be right with you, ma'am," he turned back to the blondes. "Like I was saying, they were mean and they were out for blood. I was lucky to get away with only a broken leg."

I nearly laughed out loud, but instead said sweetly, "Oh. I heard you were catching a nap in the john and when they ran an emergency fire drill, you fell off the toilet and broke your leg. Must have been real embarrassing, your bare behind sticking up in the air like that while the paramedics worked on you."

The blondes stared at me in disbelief, swiveled their heads back to him, looked at each other, and left — all without saying a single word.

He glared. "What was it you wanted, lady?"

Sometimes this psychic stuff can be a helluva lot of fun.

* * * * *

After making it real clear what a pain in the ass I was, he called back to the records room and had them print out copies of the Houston Powers case file.

I took a seat in the lobby and read through it. What a disappointment. Powers was reported missing by his mother on January 14, 1978, when he was a no-show for her forty-eighth birthday party. The follow-up was done by a detective named John Yazzie. Either Yazzie was a crummy detective or he found no evidence of foul play. No conclusions were drawn and the file was held open. That was it. No body. No suspects. Nothing but his rental car, found abandoned way out on the reservation.

Poor Houston. How was I going to tell him that not only was the murderer never caught, nobody was even looking for one?

"Awright, you illiterate fools." He was only about five-foot-three, bulky through the chest and arms, short-cropped brown hair, and a round pleasant face — if he wasn't snarling, that is. He stood in the doorway, fists on his hips, legs spread and planted like a drill sergeant. "Who made the fatal mistake of parking in my spot?"

I was the only person in the lobby and it wasn't more than a second before his eyes lasered in on me.

Oh shit. The Chief of Police. From the look of things, one tough cookie.

I must have shrunk down at least a foot in my chair. But it didn't seem to help.

"Lady, if you don't want that hunk o' junk towed, you get yourself out there and move it. Move it. Move it." His voice rose with each syllable.

"Yes. Sir. Right away, sir." I jumped up and saluted, sending pages fluttering to the floor.

He stomped over and reached across the desk counter. "Hand me a ticket book, Barnett. This is an offense of a most serious nature."

No two ways about it; I was screwed.

As I gathered my papers from the floor, I did my best to express my sincere and utter regret. He wrote the ticket anyway, so when he handed it to me, grinning like a Cheshire cat, there was nothing else to do except take it and say:

"Thank you, Chief. Thank you very much. You'll be wanting to take your poodle to the vet in a day or two. She's been knocked up by the German shepherd down the street."

"What the...?"

I handed him my business card and made a dash for the door.

So I'm a bitch sometimes. Wanna make something of it?

* * * * *

I fretted all afternoon. How could I cushion this for Houston? He had been absolutely right. Everyone, it seems, had forgotten him. No one cared he was missing or had even taken the time to look for him. That just broke my heart.

On a more selfish note, what did it mean for me if his murder was never solved? Was I doomed to hum old Bee Gees songs for the rest of my life?

About a quarter to six, Joaquin, God's gift to women, came in to spell me. His streaked blond hair flowed behind him like a mantle. His turquoise earring matched those deep, sparkling eyes. You could drown in those eyes and love every minute of it.

"*Ciao, bella.*"

He captured my hand, turned it over and kissed the inside of my wrist like he did every day when he showed up for work. He knew what effect he had on women and worked it bigtime. While he went to hang up his buckskin jacket, I struggled to catch my breath and get my legs back under me. After two months, you'd think I'd stop acting like a teenager whenever he gave me a glance. But then, you've never seen Joaquin. So what do you know?

We'd hired him part-time to fill in whenever Chloe or I needed a break. Joaquin was a struggling artist, whose modernistic approach to the Sedona landscape was just beginning to be noticed by critics and buyers alike. Book sales took off like a rocket whenever Joaquin was behind the register. Women adored him. Men adored him. He was exotic and charming and I was damn lucky the Spirit of the Vortex was the first place he'd stopped to look for work. All the store owners in town were trying to lure him away, but we hung his pictures in the store and that was worth way more than money to a passionate, artistic soul like Joaquin. For once I'd actually read someone and got it right the first time. Chloe agreed with me a hundred percent. Do I know my stuff, or do I know my stuff?

I left Chloe and Joaquin at the store and drove towards home, trying to think of a way to tell my resident ghost he may as well unpack his suitcase. He wasn't going anywhere for a while. Dammit.

When I turned off the main road, I could see Houston sitting on the freshly painted front porch, waiting. Waiting anxiously. Waiting desperately.

I turned around. Okay, so I'm a coward.

Another ten minutes down the road, I saw the sign for Slide Rock State Park, turned in, and pulled up to the ranger's booth. The park ranger came out and I tried not to stare. Was it male? Or was it female? The person was short and squatty and the uniform added to a classic study in androgyny.

"We're closin' up in twenty minutes, ma'am."

"That's okay, Miss. I just wanted to take a quick look around." I smiled, confident in my choice of gender, until I noticed the name tag: Bruce.

He cleared his throat gruffly and shoved a brochure through the window. "Yeah, well, 'Miss.' I won't charge you the admission fee this time. Just be out of the park by six-thirty."

Once again I'm amazed at the dead-on accuracy of my marvelous sixth sense. Forget what I said about Joaquin. It was probably just luck of the draw.

I parked the car and walked down to the creek, passing the original settlers' home kept up by the State. The angle of the late afternoon sun wrapped the weathered stone in a warm haze.

Down by Slide Rock ancient pink boulders were polished smooth by the rushing water. I sighed and drank in the beauty like a good Bordeaux as, perched on a big flat rock, sun dappling through the cottonwood trees, I watched the last diehard family drag their screaming kids out of the water and make for the parking lot.

For the twenty years I lived with Andrew the Anus, every day at five forty-five in the afternoon a knot would form at the base of my neck in dread of the jackass walking in the front door. No matter how hard I tried to be in a good mood. No matter how much positive reinforcement I bolstered myself with during the day, he always managed to bring me down with some poisoned remark. If not about me, about one of our friends or someone he worked with. That knot was back. But as I sat there wondering what to do about Houston, even my lump of tension had to give in to the peaceful tranquility of this special place.

There was no doubt about it. Someone had to help the poor guy cross over. It looked like I'd have to turn psychic detective after all.

* * * * *

Suddenly it is pitch friggin' black. Hey! Who turned off the lights? And I can see my breath in the night air. Cold. Winter? How can it be winter? Snow crunches beneath my feet as I pace — waiting. Who am I waiting for? The full moon reflects off the rushing water. The cold wind lifts my hair, moaning eerily through the trees. I glance at my watch. Eleven-thirty. Nearly the witching hour. Somehow I know there's danger. I run in slow motion back to my car. And now I'm driving. Faster and faster.

I am so friggin' scared I can't think straight. My car fishtails around the bend. The beams of my headlights careen wildly over the twisting roadway...

"Miss? Miss? You have to leave now."

I jerked around. The sun silhouetted the ranger. I was never so glad to be kicked out of a place in my whole life.

* * * * *

I pulled into my driveway and shut off the engine. Before I could even get the keys out of the ignition Houston materialized in my lap.

"Tell me! For God's sake, tell me."

Oh, yuck — ghost slime. This was too weird. "First, get the hell off my lap. Then we'll have show and tell. I'll show you mine. You tell me yours."

Houston vanished from my lap. And reappeared beside me as I got out of the car and walked up to the house.

"What did you find out?" He was chomping at the bit.

"I'll tell you everything. But first, you tell me. What does Slide Rock have to do with your murder?"

"Oh my God! You really are psychic. Slide Rock. Even talking about it scares the bejeezus out of me."

I knew what he meant. It scared the bejeezus out of me too. But I kept my mouth shut and my ears open. I needed to know everything he could tell me about what happened. I'd decided to take the case, to help him cross over...

Chapter Five

...if I could.

God knows, it wouldn't be easy. Mobsters. Land scams. Car bombs, heavy shit. Mario Puzo stuff. To say I was totally stressed out would be like telling you George Clooney is drop-dead gorgeous — I mean, come on, it goes without saying. Right?

I don't handle stress well. A doctor once prescribed Prozac to help me, you know, "take the edge off." But the pills gave me migraines, and chocolate works so much better that I flushed the Prozac and doubled up on Milky Way bars.

That day was particularly stressful. With Haggis hot on my heels, I marched straight into the kitchen, opened the fridge which contained three cans of Diet Pepsi, an apple just about ready for folk art, an orange that no longer was, and a bag of Hershey's Almond Kisses. I grabbed the bag and began a journey into its depths while Haggis drooled on my shoes.

A dozen wrappers later, Houston commented: "You don't watch it, you're gonna have a butt like a Buick."

"Thank you, Mister I'm-so-tactful." I popped another one in my mouth. "And I thought I left that chauvinist crap back in Chicago with the Anus. Silly me."

"Sorry." And he sounded like he really was. "Guy was a real asshole, huh?"

"If you want to see my ex, look up 'asshole' in the dictionary. His picture is on that page."

"Puckered and pink?"

I put the Kisses back in the fridge. "Oh, you've met. I didn't even know how miserable I was until I got away from him. Would you believe I used to live on lettuce and water?" Okay, I was exaggerating, but not much. "Spent hours on the friggin'

Stairmaster. Sweated my ass off in the sauna. All so he could say his wife was a perfect size six."

"Nothing wrong with a size six."

I lifted my chin, daring him to disagree. "Eight is better and I'm shooting for a ten."

"Good plan."

I snagged a Diet Pepsi. Isn't irony just the soul of humor? "I didn't learn anything today. The police report is a dead end."

His face fell.

"But I've decided to take the case." I snapped my heels and saluted. "Tildy MacNamara, Detective to the Dead, at your service. Granted it's a somewhat limited field. And the dead are notoriously slow to pay, but what the hell."

He looked like he might start crying any second.

"I was only kidding."

If he was this bummed because the only person who could help him solve this thing and get on with eternity was a complete drooling idiot, it was definitely better not to tell him that no one even knew he'd been murdered. If he burst into tears, I'd have to comfort him, which meant — oooh gross — touching and, well — we definitely didn't want him to burst into tears. Distracting him was worth a try.

And whaddya know, hot damn. Whistling and snapping my fingers worked like a charm — just like with Haggis, which gave me the opportunity to ask: "What happened at Slide Rock?"

He shuddered, "Slide Rock," then folded himself into a lotus position, levitating about three feet off the floor. He appeared to be settling in for the long haul. So, I pulled one of my own new ladderback chairs away from my own new table, white French country to contrast the robin's-egg blue ceramic counter top and clear beveled-glass-door cabinets. Andrew would have hated it, too bourgeois, but then Andrew didn't have anything to do with it. Andrew didn't have anything to do with anything of mine — not anymore. I sat down to listen to Houston's tale.

"Almost immediately after the car bombing, investigators zeroed in on this guy John Harvey Adamson. He gave up Max Dunlap and James Robison. Last I heard, Adamson was in the witness protection program. Dunlap and Robison had been convicted of murder but not sentenced."

I was confused. "Wait a minute. They already had the guys?"

"Yeah, but not a single one of us believed the conspiracy stopped with them. We knew it went a lot higher. And it stands to reason you know, if they were the only ones, then why was I killed?"

"Good point." Now don't get scared, but I think I was beginning to get it. "So why did the IRE send you up here?"

"I came up following a lead on Ted Cochran and the Canyon State Land and Cattle Company."

"Ted Cochran of Cochran's Paradise Resort? You're kidding. He bought one of Joaquin's landscapes for the resort lobby."

Evidently Houston didn't give a rat's ass about Cochran's love of fine art. He ignored me and went on. "Word was, Cochran and his partners were fronting a land scam for the mob. I knew in my gut that Ted Cochran was dirty. But none of my leads panned out and I couldn't prove it."

"Wow. A crook. I just saw him at the art festival at Tlaquepaque last week. You wouldn't believe how bad his hair plugs look."

"Do you want to hear this or not?"

"Sorry." I zipped my lips.

"When the Arizona Project was over, a series of forty-six articles was published in magazines and newspapers around the world. We did the best we could, but we couldn't catch what Bolles had been chasing.

"That year, I decided to spend the Christmas holidays in Sedona with a friend. Somebody got nervous and I started getting death threats. Never could resist a good byline, so I started nosing around again. Then on New Year's Eve I get an anonymous phone call. This disguised voice says meet him out at Slide Rock. Says he's got something gonna blow my investigation wide open."

I looked at him incredulously. "Oh no. You went? You fell for that old con?"

"Yeah, baby. Hook, line and sinker. I said I was a good reporter. I never said I was a *smart* reporter."

I prodded. "And...?"

"It was nighttime. So cold I could see my breath. The full moon shone through the naked tree branches. The wind was moaning. I tell ya, it was like something out of a Steven King novel."

"Yeah. Yeah, Ichabod Crane. I know all that. I saw it too, remember?"

"Then why the hell did you ask me?"

"Geez. Touchy."

"Like I *started* to say...," Such an attitude. "...I parked and walked up to Slide Rock. Nobody was there."

"Big surprise."

He glared at me. "After an hour it dawned on me how stupid the whole thing was. I mean, I was supposed to be on vacation, for chrissake. So, I headed back to town. The first bend in the road and Mr. Genius Ace Reporter realizes somebody's cut his brake lines."

"Yikes! You're kidding."

Encouraged, he went on. "You drive that road, Tildy. You know how dangerous it is. It's a bloody roller coaster. The car picked up speed and got harder and harder to control. I had to do something fast or I'd end up like Don Bolles."

"Duh. You did."

"Know-it-all. On an upgrade I managed to plow the car off into a gravel pile left over from a road crew. I just sat there. Man, I was shaking like a leaf. But I was still alive. Still breathing. The car wouldn't start up again. The goddamn oil pan was shattered.

"I started off down the road, paranoid as hell — when out of nowhere this car comes screaming around the curve."

I closed my eyes and the nightmare was back, pulling me in.

His voice made it even more real. "I was a deer caught in the headlights. My heart was a jackhammer pounding in my throat."

So was mine.

"I turned to run but..."

My legs won't move. The lights are everywhere, blinding me. Now it's too late and I cry out...

WHAM — *then the scraping, the digging, and the dirt on my face.*

I opened my eyes, took a deep breath and steadied myself. "Holy shit. They buried us alive."

He was out-of-breath too (if ghosts can be). He tried to steady himself. "Us? Well, I don't know about you, Tildy. But yeah, I was alive when I went into the ground."

I felt the tears starting. "That's horrible. I'm so sorry, Houston."

"Tell me about it." He cleared his throat gruffly. "Anyway, I've been tethered to this place for almost a quarter century."

"Hmm. I'll bet you're buried out in the orchard."

He looked at me. "You think?"

Then we both looked out the window where the moon created a shadowy netherworld beneath the trees.

Without looking back at me, he asked, "Got a shovel?"

Chapter Six

"I bet you say that to all the girls."

It was a cinch in his current condition Houston couldn't handle a shovel. So, it looked like Tildy the Tool-Time Gal once more to the rescue.

I dug holes out in the damn apple orchard until almost dawn. I did find one skeleton, but it was the wrong species — feline not *Homo sapiens*. I carefully reburied it. I had to stop then and take Haggis back to the house, because he kept digging the pitiful thing back up. The work was exhausting with no reward except a few old boots, a pile of buried trash, and a box with old photographs. Every time I tried to call it quits, my own personal pep squad showed up to cheer me on. The sadistic bastard.

* * * * *

Even under the hot shower my muscles were already cramping up. I made a mental note to call Pam of the Magic Fingers and set up an extra massage. But right now I had to hustle my butt and get dressed because Grace was coming by at eight to pick me up.

I had just finished combing my hair when Houston popped in.

"Have you ever considered going blonde?"

"Been there. Done that. I was a blonde for twenty years." All those hours in the salon trying to be beautiful and the jerk dumped me anyway. My declaration of independence was turning that long silky blonde mane into a short red curly bob. "Andrew loves blondes. In the Biblical sense."

"Ooops. Faux pas. There's a lot to be said for graying redheads."

"You're smarter than you look."

Houston tilted his head and studied me. "But a good cut would work wonders."

I splayed my fingers and raised them to his face, "Talk to the hand." Grabbing my purse, I headed down the stairs.

Grace called up through the screen door, "Burning gas and daylight. You ready or not?"

"Coming."

Houston hovered beside me. "Going out?"

"Ah-huh." Who did he think he was? My mother? Forget I said that. My mother never cared where I went or what I did. Always said she "trusted me." What the hell was that supposed to mean?

"Be gone long?"

There would be no quick get away this time. "Grace and I are going to Flagstaff for supplies."

Grace was standing on the edge of the porch , staring out at the orchard.

He floated on down ahead of me to wedge himself halfway-in, halfway-out the screen door so he could have a good look at her.

"Oh, so that's Grace. Nice hair."

"Shut up," I hissed and slammed the door on him. Literally.

"Here I am. Sorry you had to wait. It's been a helluva morning."

She turned, a funny expression on her face. "What's going on out in the orchard?"

"What do you mean?"

"You looking for something? There's a shit-load of holes out there."

"Holes? What holes?" I leaned over the rail and squinted. "Son of a gun. Must be gophers." If I looked at her, I'd burst out laughing.

As we walked to the car, Houston popped out of a tree. "Be home by dark. We have a lot to talk about."

Oh swell. Maybe I should have thought about checking into a motel.

* * * * *

After spending the morning at Sam's Club loading up on supplies for both Death By Chocolate and Spirit of the Vortex, Grace and I stopped for lunch on the way out of town at Buster's.

I ordered this incredible fettuccine Alfredo with extra garlic bread. I mean, God forbid Houston couldn't nag me about my big fat ass.

Grace picked at her shrimp Louie. For her size, she ate like a bird. But then I saw how it was with her. She was saving herself for dessert. Did I say "dessert?" I meant DESSERT! Over coffee we sampled and critiqued three luscious chocolate concoctions: Chocolate Fantasy Mousse, the Triple-Layer German Chocolate Cake and their White Chocolate Raspberry Cheesecake.

Grace dabbed at the corner of her mouth with a crisp linen napkin. "I've been thinking of hanging some of Joaquin's paintings in my store."

That surprised me. "Really?"

She grinned back at me. "Maybe if I did, he'd come around more often. God, he's got such a nice butt." She flexed her fingers. "Firm. Round."

Oookay. At fifty-one Grace was ten years older than I, but obviously Joaquin's ass didn't have anything to do with age.

She flexed her fingers again.

"Grace," I said. "Don't squeeze the Charmin."

"Party pooper."

I turned my palm up. "Did he ever...?" I made kissing noises.

Grace nearly swooned. "Oh my God, did he ever."

"Can you imagine being married to him?"

"Me? Oh honey, I can't imagine being married to anybody. My momma didn't raise no fool."

I must have winced, because she immediately patted my hand. "Oh, Tildy, I didn't mean..."

I tried not to recoil as the heat snaked up my arm. If there wasn't a fire — and Grace said there wasn't — then why did I flash on one every time I touched her? Maybe I wasn't seeing her past. Maybe I was seeing her future. Oh, shit. How do you tell your friend it looks like she might buy the farm in a five-alarm fire? Good question. And I didn't know the answer, not yet, anyway.

* * * * *

When I got home, Haggis came running to meet me and jumped in my arms. I'm pretty sure if he hadn't, Houston would have. They were both all over me as I headed up the stairs. "Where have you been? Good grief, I thought you'd never get back. We've got to get to work."

"Cool your jets. I'm hot. I'm tired. First things, first. Get your priorities straight, honey."

He shot back, "There's nothing wrong with my priorities, honey."

All the same, he stayed out of my face through a shower, a pint of Rocky Road, and a rousing round of *Jeopardy*. I like Trebek better with a moustache. More dashing. Don't you think?

Houston couldn't take it another second. "Now? Please."

Truth be known, I had no inclination to do this — and I told him straight out. "I've never done anything like this before. Not even close."

"That's okay. I have."

"So you're willing to risk your eternity on me?"

He nodded.

I swallowed. "But what if I'm not?"

"You can do it, Tildy. I know you can. You're smart and you're gutsy..."

Who the hell was he talking about, anyway? I looked around, but there were only two of us in the room — if you count him. Me? Gutsy? Yeah, right.

He went on. "...you can do whatever you set your mind to. You'll be a helluva detective. And I'm just the guy to teach you how to unravel a mystery."

I opened the drawer in the lamp table, grabbed a pencil and a pad, curled my feet up under me and said, "Okay, I'm game if you are. Shoot."

The words came spewing out of him like pea soup out of Linda Blair. Did I just say that? Holy smoke, I was already turning into Raymond Chandler. Fuggeddaboutit.

I tried to keep up as he rattled off all this info about newspaper morgues, police reports, the value of live interviews and on and on and on. He knew what he was talking about. And it was a damned good thing because, like I said, as far as I was concerned Colonel Mustard did it in the dining room with the candelabra. In other words....

Chapter Seven

...I didn't have a *Clue*. And it looked like nobody in Sedona did either. The *Red Rock News* carried a whole paragraph on Houston's disappearance — big wow.

Okay. Next.

I ran a computer search at the library and turned up Houston's *World News Magazine* series on the terrorist. It was a masterpiece worthy of the Pulitzer.

There was also a small article when he disappeared without a trace after participating in the Bolles investigation — but that was it. Nothing that would help me find his murderer. I made copies of everything to show Houston. At least he'd know he was missed. And maybe his trained eye would find something I didn't.

Then I went home and spent some time online, and turned up a bunch of stuff about the Don Bolles murder, including the fact that Max Dunlap and James Robison were still alive. I tapped into *The Arizona Republic* website. Their online archives didn't go back that far; the older stuff was stored on microfiche at their headquarters. I'd have to make a trip to Phoenix.

Houston wasn't "hanging around" anywhere, so I left the articles on the table where he'd find them, and a note that I was going to Phoenix to see what I could dig up.

I packed up Haggis and his little tartan-plaid suitcase, and headed for the bookstore. He was going to bunk in with Chloe while I was gone. They were best buds and I knew she'd take good care of him, but I was still a little anxious. In the six months we'd been together, I'd never left the little guy for more than a few hours. This time I'd be gone at least a couple of days, and if I got on a hot trail, well, who knew.

Chloe arched one well-plucked brow as she thumbed through the four pages of doggie instructions I gave her — especially when she came to the homeopathic all-natural diet. "What the hell is he? The reincarnation of the Dalai Lama?"

"I'm a nervous mother," I shrugged. "So shoot me."

*****

As I drove the interstate from Sedona to Phoenix, the temperature climbed from 88 to 115. Waves of heat rippled across the pavement like restless spirits. I cranked the air-conditioner down to Arctic freeze and forged ahead.

In the heart of Phoenix, I found the Arizona Biltmore, maneuvered the 4Runner up the elegant drive to the front and handed my keys to the flirtatious valet — little did he know I was old enough to be his... uh... older sister.

The instant I got out of the car, the sun scorched my fair skin. I'd have a swell crop of new freckles in the morning. When I inhaled, the very air seared my lungs. And I was immediately drenched in sweat — but no worries. As they say in Arizona: "It's a dry heat."

If you're crazy enough to come to Phoenix in the summer, you can get any hotel room in town for half price or better, and little old frugal me could stay at the legendary Arizona Biltmore for a song. I love a bargain.

Inside, everything was slick and polished, cool and elegant. Wood, stone and marble. Frank Lloyd Wright's fingerprints were all over this place, right down to the circa fifties modern furniture.

My room was spacious, plush and comfy — as deluxe a hotel as I've ever seen, and I've seen a few. Good old Andrew always made sure we stayed in the most expensive, most prestigious accommodations available — the pretentious prick.

After a swim, a six-inch-tall club sandwich, and a white wine spritzer, I got dressed and headed over to the *Arizona Republic* on Van Buren. It was a humongous ten story glass building in downtown Phoenix.

The lobby receptionist directed me to the Archive Department where a nice lady named Stella sat me down in front of a computer and explained how their program worked.

Houston's words echoed in my mind: Always start at the beginning.

It took a good hour to scour the database for articles pertaining to the Don Bolles incident — another hour to print them all out. We're talking about a series of newsworthy events stretching all the way from that terrible day in June so long ago, until now. Reporters and investigators are still scratching their heads trying to put together what really happened back in 1976.

It was no wonder Bolles was rubbed out. He'd stirred up a real hornet's nest, exposing everybody from high-powered politicians involved in land scams all the way to lowlife slimebags who were rigging dog races. And it was all there in the *Arizona Republic* for the world to know: how a man named Max Dunlap allegedly hired John Harvey Adamson to silence Don Bolles who exposed the illegal activities of his mentor, Kemper Marley. Marley was allegedly into crime bigtime, both organized and disorganized. Could be he was worried about being exposed and decided to have Bolles silenced. I might have been able to reach him but wasn't sure I wanted to, since he had died in 1990.

Adamson admitted to planting the bomb on Bolles' white Datsun. He then rolled over on Dunlap and a guy named James Robison, a Chandler plumber who, according to Adamson, was the trigger man. Over the next twenty years, these three men were tried, released, re-tried, convicted, judgments overturned, re-tried, acquitted and on and on and on. It was a convoluted pile of legal manure.

Was Houston connected to any of these people? Maybe not. Probably not. But, back at the beginning of 1978 when Houston was murdered, this whole thing was a boiling cauldron of murder and conspiracy. These men had everything to lose and you know what they say: Desperate men do desperate things. It was as good a place to start as any.

I went back to the Biltmore, kicked off my shoes, sprawled across the cushy bed, and spent the rest of the day with a smart, tenacious pit bull of a reporter named Don Bolles who didn't deserve such a horrible death.

* * * * *

About seven-thirty I put on my slinky black pant suit, my diamond studs, and (believe it or not) a pair of three-inch pumps and went downstairs with every intention of treating myself to a sensible dinner in one of the hotel's excellent restaurants. Wouldn't you know it? I was waylaid by a sign at the door of a lavish conference room advising the world that the Republican Party Ladies' Auxiliary was holding their annual fundraiser Chocolate Buffet.

Any thought of a sensible dinner went right out of my head as I inhaled and nearly swooned on the excellent aroma of everything under the sun made of chocolate.

What else could I do? I went in, did my civic duty, and furthered Houston's cause in the process. The hostess-with-the-mostess (and I do mean "mostess" — her cup size had to be at least a "G" — I mean we're talking wheelbarrow time here, folks) was none other than Ellen Johnson, ex-wife of the honorable Senator Wade Johnson. She was sixty if she was a day, but the plastic surgeon had done his work well — several times if the taut, shiny skin and the constant surprised expression on her face were any indication.

The good senator just happened to be one of the folks Bolles implicated in the seventies land scam. His family were Arizona pioneers who made their fortune in cattle and real estate over the years. It was speculated that the wealthy, powerful Johnsons had strong mob ties and that Wade's Senate seat was bought and paid for with dirty money. Now, if somebody got you a nice job like U.S. Senator, wouldn't you do anything you could to pay them back? Even if it meant scamming Native Americans out of their ancestral lands? Sure you would. Right? Wrong.

Ellen Johnson pumped my hand enthusiastically as she accepted my donation check with the other. "I'm so pleased you could make it, Ms. MacNamara. I can't imagine how your name was ever left off the invitation list. Hope you can see your way clear to forgive our little boo-boo."

She leaned forward graciously and I worried her big "boo-boos" were going to fall out of her dress any second. "No problem, Mrs. Johnson."

"Please, dear," she snagged a roving waiter and lifted a martini off his tray while I accepted a flute of champagne. "Call me Ellen. I haven't answered to Mrs. Johnson for quite a while."

I ate chocolate, drank champagne and hung out with Ellen Johnson, all the while encouraging her to drink up. I figured if she got a little tight, she might get a little loose. She did, but it backfired. I wanted loose lips to find out everything I could about Johnson's possible involvement in what I was beginning to think of as "my case." But what I got was loosey-goosey — as in goosing the busboy whose acne-inflamed adolescent face grew even redder as she pinched and groped. She giggled and ogled and gave him her phone number. He looked at me with panic in his eyes and made a bee-line for the kitchen while I steered her away. Four too many martinis had made a fool out of the poor woman. I offered to drive her home in her new black Mercedes S600 — what the hell. I'm the one that got her drunk.

It didn't go well. I took a wrong turn — surprised? It seems we went west instead of east, south instead of north and wound up in an area inhabited by junkies, the homeless and the lost. Like me.

I stopped at a red light and had a look around. It was beyond dirty. Litter everywhere. The sidewalks were cracked and broken up like an earthquake had just hit. The bars, strip joints and run down shacks were so dilapidated I think the graffiti was the only thing holding them up. On the corner a couple of drunks played tug-of-war over a bottle.

Hmmm. "Oh, Ellen?"

She rolled her head around and squinted at me.

"Do you know where we are? How do I get to your house from here?"

At that moment, a fire engine red Chevy Impala low-rider pulled up beside us. The front end danced the rumba to the radio's pounding salsa beat. Inside, the four macho Latinos looked over and — woe is me — caught Ellen's eye.

She literally hung out the open window, exposing her humongous breasts, bellowing, "Anybody up for a gang bang?"

Oh boy.

I grabbed the back of her gown and pulled. Of course the delicate fabric ripped completely off and there she was, in all her glory.

The Chicanos stared in absolute amazement while Ellen flexed her pecs and made her breasts dance in rhythm to the radio. Even the drunks on the sidewalk stopped fighting to have a look at this unusual display.

What can you do?

I shrugged and smiled sheepishly as I leaned forward and called pleasantly, "You boys know how to get back to Paradise Valley from here?"

Ellen toppled out the window and landed in a heap on the pavement.

The stud behind the wheel gawked in total disbelief, "Aye, Diós."

All four of them hopped out of the car. As I debated whether to drive away and leave her, the boys hauled her up and loaded her in the back seat.

"Holy shit, lady. You should take better care of your mom."

Don't even bother, Tildy. "You're absolutely right," I said. "I was taking Mom home to tuck her in bed and I took a wrong turn." I'll say!

They did give me some damn good directions and within a half hour, I was helping Ellen, a.k.a. Mom, into bed. Her house was a showcase — exactly what you'd expect from a woman whose identity was built on who she used to be.

I found a phone in the den and called a taxi. While I waited, I wandered around. The walls were covered with "trophy" photos of Wade and Ellen and people we all know. Good old Charles Keating and Wade and Ellen — bet they got their investment out before the S&L blew up. Alice Cooper in full make-up with Ellen Johnson as an accessory. Glen Campbell and Wade Johnson in cowboy regalia and...

"Oh my God." I moved in for a closer look. "Grace?"

In the photo a small group of people gathered around a sign that announced: "Future site of Cochran's Paradise Resort" — a ground-breaking ceremony among the famous Sedona red rocks. One of the dozen or so in the picture was a much younger Grace. She was partially hidden behind the sign. But it was her alright.

"You sly dog. You never said you ran in such powerful circles."

She was there with Wade and Ellen Johnson (whose cup size was decidedly smaller), Ted Cochran, and others I didn't know.

Hadn't Houston said that Cochran was fronting a land scam for the mob? The same mob that Wade Johnson was tight with? Hmmm.

Doors were opening....

Chapter Eight

...with a CLANK!

The town of Florence squats outside the Arizona State Prison main gates. To the people of Florence, the prison is what the car industry is to Detroit. They live it, eat it, and sleep it, and they don't get much company outside rattlesnakes, scorpions, and prison groupies. The penitentiary is a fortress set smack in the middle of this hell. It's cement and barbed wire, a looming, intimidating institution, even if you're on the righteous side of the barbed wire.

I got there at nine and the visitor gate didn't open until ten, but I was still twenty cars back in line. Who knew it was going to be like Bargain Days at Macy's. What? Were they giving away something free?

An hour later the light bulb went off. It was taking so long because of heavy security. The guards went over my car like they'd gone over every single car that came through the gates. Top to bottom and back again. Then they went over me. I held up the line at the metal detector because the brass buttons on my incredibly dignified royal blue suit kept setting the damn thing off — so much for credibility. Finally the matron resorted to a body search. Ellen would have loved it, but it made me queasy and I fought the urge to run. Even though they didn't confiscate my contraband Baby Ruth bar, it had been mauled by so many sweaty hands, even I wouldn't eat it.

By the time we were let into the waiting room the Baby Ruth, half melted and smooshed against the wrapper, was doing a lot better than I was. The swamp cooler blew straight down from the ceiling. It was as muggy as August in Chicago, and I fervently wished I'd gone with shorts and a tank top and said to hell with the suit. Oh, and did I mention that my pantyhose were soakin wet and clinging like cellophane to all the places I shouldn't tug at? Well, they were — and I did anyway.

Wondering if my hair had morphed into its Shirley Temple mode, I collapsed on a bench and had a look around. There were already at least fifty people in the waiting room. Cramped. Sweaty. Phew! Somebody find a can of Glade, quick!

Children shrieked and chased each other. Some babies cried. Some nursed at their mothers' breasts. A heavy-set Indian woman spread a picnic on a Navajo blanket. Young tired-looking women checked their watches while older folks waited stoically.

The need for strict security was a given, and I got it — no question. But how sad that these folks had to endure being herded and penned like cattle just to visit the people they love. It was a horrible place, a place of dwindling hope and lost dreams.

A little after noon they called my name. I hurried after the guard into a stark room partitioned by Plexiglas and steel.

"Max Dunlap." He pointed. "Number four."

I went over, sat down and waited, wondering what he would be like. I had never met a convicted murderer before — who has?

They say Kemper Marley had taken Dunlap under his wing all those years ago. Rumor was there were three people on their hit list. Bolles, of course. Also, Bruce Babbit, State Attorney General, and Al "King Alphonso," a penny-ante thug with a big mouth. The other two lucked out. Bolles didn't.

Marley's supposed empire had been far-reaching — bookmaking for the mob, election tampering, dogtrack rigging, running illegal aliens, land fraud — and that was just the tip of the iceberg. Not a very nice man, and Dunlap had studied at his knee.

But the man who walked in wasn't De Niro or James Gandolfini or even Joe Pesci; he was just a heavy-set older guy in an orange prison jumpsuit shuffling over to sit down on the opposite side of the glass. His watery blue eyes sized me up, narrowing in appreciation.

He picked up the phone.

I did the same. I wasn't getting any vibes from him. I'd probably never know whether he arranged to have Don Bolles blown to smithereens or if he was framed like a lot of people seemed to think. That was okay with me. I didn't want to relive that scene. Thank you very much.

"Well damn, they told me that there was a writer here to see me, but they never said you were so pretty." He raked his fingers through his thinning gray hair.

Just my luck. The first guy in a long time to think I'm a babe was a hard-up seventy-year-old lifer with questionable eyesight.

"And they didn't tell me you were such a charmer, Mister Dunlap." As they say in the Valley: Gag me with a spoon.

"Charmer, eh?" He shot a stream of brown evil-looking goop into a paper cup. I resisted the urge to make a face. "Every couple of years someone comes around wanting a story from me. What's your angle?"

I was ready for him. "Everybody's always writing about the Bolles murder. I'm coming at it from another direction. I'm writing a book about the I.R.E."

He got this blank look on his face, but I went on anyway.

"What do you know about the disappearance of a reporter named Houston Powers?"

"Never heard of him." He leaned forward. "But even if I had, I wouldn't say." He spit again.

He was puking me out. Where the hell was all that stuff coming from? The wad in his cheek wasn't getting any smaller.

He lowered his voice confidentially, "I was wrongly convicted, ya know."

"No!" Where did I put that violin?

He went on, "So, I can't say a lot. The appeals process and all."

"You're working on an appeal?"

He nodded.

"Another one?" I gasped. "This makes how many?"

He grinned. "It never hurts to give it one more shot."

Can't blame a guy for trying. Or can you? "That makes sense," I said, "but if I can't get my story from you, where am I going to get it? Kemper Marley is dead. So is Neal Roberts, the attorney. John Harvey Adamson is..."

"...dead," he interrupted. "And I'm glad." His hate and frustration lent bitter credence to his argument of being set-up. "That sorry sumbitch could have let me off the hook before he kicked the bucket. But noooo. I ain't sitting around mourning that one. Hmm-mmm."

I cleared my throat and squirmed in my chair. "All righty then. What about this other guy? Robison? Would he know anything?"

"I can't say what he knows, except he was innocent too."

"Oh. Really?"

"Jimmy? Hell, yes. Didn't you hear? He was visiting his sick old gray-haired mother in Kansas." He spit again. "But he wouldn't talk to you either."

"If he's innocent, why not?"

"He knows which side his bread is buttered on. He came into a windfall a few years back," he winked broadly, "smart guy parlayed it into some really big money."

I hesitated to ask, "Windfall?"

"Well, you know."

"Yeah." I thought I did know. Translation: hush money.

"So now he's living la vida loca south of the border."

La vida loca, eh? "Must have been some windfall."

"You bet your cute little ass it was."

Cute *little* ass? I'd have to remember to tell Houston what a marvelous guy this Max Dunlap was — I mean, aside from being convicted of cold-blooded murder and all, he was definitely a man who knew a fine specimen of womanhood when he saw it.

"You can't think of anybody I could talk to about this?"

"Well, there might be this one guy...."

I jumped on it like a dog on a bone. "Yeah?"

"He used to be a serious player, but that was then. This is now. Guy's so old, maybe he's forgotten his own name, but you could look him up. See what he knows."

I drove straight back to the Arizona Biltmore, tossed those sweat-soaked panty hose in the trash, and showered away the day, the prison and everything that went with it.

* * * * *

Dunlap had given me the address for some dude named Joseph Attanasio. He'd whispered the name, glancing around nervously the whole time. But that wasn't what bothered me — it was the way he was laughing his ass off when he left to go back to his cell.

Attanasio's neighborhood was a lush oasis in the middle of the desert. His "digs" covered a whole city block. The graceful two-story white hacienda was covered in ivy and red mission tile. The doors and windows had intricately carved wrought iron bars that probably weren't there just for looks. A six-car garage was around the corner in the back and next to it was a guest house that dwarfed my own pretty gingerbread house.

I cruised by at slow speed and whistled. "Wow!"

I pulled into the circular drive and — oh my God — found myself staring at a rose garden that would put the White House to shame. The bushes lined the walkway to the front door in a rainbow of petals. Two Hispanic men toiled under the blazing sun pruning, trimming and watering. And they were doing a hell of a job. Old Joe needed to give them a raise.

As I lifted the brass knocker on the massive oak doors, I wondered if anyone would mind if I picked a few. Suddenly the door was jerked open and a tall buxom redhead barreled into me and knocked me on my ass.

With one hand, she held together her torn nurse's uniform. In the other she clutched a small dead animal. Not seeming the least bit sorry, she stared down at me and snarled, "Excuse me," then stomped off down the drive.

Well, I have had more sincere apologies. You know, like the one just before they smash your boob in the vice for a mammogram. And just as believable.

I was managing to get my feet under me when — bam! Some moron in a wheelchair sends me headlong into the rose bushes.

"Yeow!"

The moron in the wheelchair was older than God. Mister Attanasio, I presume. He yelled after the redhead, "And don't come crawling back, baby. You give real sorry enemas anyway." He had this drawl, and the wheezing and the breathing apparatus made him sound kinda like Darth Vader.

Maybe he could use the Force to get my prickly ass out of the rose bushes. "Help?"

The old man stared at me a moment, then wheezed, "Fuck off." He wheeled himself back into the house and slammed the door.

"And may the Force be with you too, asshole."

The gardeners pulled me bleeding and whimpering from the rose bushes. They helped me pick the enormous thorns out of my butt, chattering and laughing the whole time. I wish to God I spoke Spanish. I'll never know what they said about my "cute little ass". One good thing, I never heard the word Buick come up in the conversation.

After they loaded me into my car, I fell back to replot my strategy.

About a block down the street, the redhead stomped along the sidewalk. I pulled up next to her and let down the window. "Need a ride?"

She must have thought I looked pretty harmless because she walked over and got in the car.

She sat there, nurse's cap askew, bodice shredded and clutched to her bosom, and took a good look at me: bleeding, hair sticking out in all directions, clothes torn and dirty.

"What the hell happened to you?" she demanded.

Helluva bedside manner, this one. I wondered if it was true about the enemas.

After that swell sendoff from Attanasio, it was pretty obvious he wasn't going to be the easiest guy to get next to. Maybe Florence Nightingale here could point me in the right direction. I put the car in "park," turned toward her and smiled, "You first."

She was mad as a wet hen... "That nasty old lecher. Who does he think he is? You know, I get sick and tired of these assholes who think just because they've got a little money, it entitles them to do or say whatever they want."...and she was on a roll. "You know, the agency tried to warn me about this old coot. He's gone through a half-dozen nurses in less than a month." She shook the dead animal at me. And now I could see it was a short poofy black wig. "The maniac thinks he's Elvis. Well, I got news for him. The King would never treat a girl like that. No job is worth him putting his cold, clammy paws on me."

Elvis, huh? Well thank you, ma'am. Thank you very much. So, the old goat liked to chase nurses, did he? Hmmm. Like my mama always said: The way to a man's heart is...

Chapter Nine

...through his scrotum.

Promptly at six-thirty that evening, I stood in front of those massive oak doors the second time that day. After adjusting the bobby pins holding on my nurse's cap, shifting the padding in my "Wonder Bra," and making sure the seams in my white stockings were straight, I once again lifted the lion's head knocker.

A gorilla in a Polo shirt and golf shorts answered the door. At least he looked like a gorilla. He was about six-foot-five, three hundred pounds and covered in thick fur.

I smiled and threw back my shoulders. Even in the Wonder Bra I had a hell of a long way to go to match the busty redhead. "I'm from the agency."

He just stared at me.

"I have an appointment."

Still nothing. I resisted the urge to snap my fingers in front of his face. "You know. With Mr. Attanasio?"

He finally seemed to come out of his coma, grunted, turned around, and walked away.

I followed, noticing that his knuckles nearly scraped the floor. Like I said, a gorilla.

He lead me across the black marble foyer through a labyrinth of hallways which opened onto enormous rooms full of art and antiques. An entire wing was dedicated to nothing but Elvis paraphernalia. I mean to say, room after room. This guy had more of the King's stuff than Elvis ever did.

Posters, records, photographs, tee-shirts, dinnerware — everything Elvis. One display case housed at least a hundred of those stupid bobbing-head Elvis dolls. A pedestal held a diamond pinky ring in the shape of a huge "E" under glass just like the Crown Jewels.

We passed through a mock showroom complete with cocktail tables and dummy fans. On the stage, two Elvises preened. One was fat, wearing one of those ridiculous white jumpsuits with a wide leather belt encrusted with gemstones. The other was what I like to refer to as "my Elvis". A rock-and-roll Elvis. Sexy as hell in head-to-toe black. They both looked so real I stopped to stare and nearly peed my pants when the band blared to life and Elvis did a duet with himself: *I'm just a hunka hunka burning love. A hunka hunka burning love.*

This Attanasio character needed to get a grip; but it was a pretty good setup all the same. Madam Tussaud would have been green with envy.

The next room was dedicated to this big old high-finned pink Cadillac convertible. Behind it, a fully lit marquee blinked: "Elvis Starring In *The Trouble With Girls.*"

I'm telling you, it was all pretty freakin' amazing.

But you ain't heard nothing yet.

Then we came to the bathroom. The motif was, get this, *Blue Hawaii* with Elvis crooning in the background. You got your fake palm trees everywhere, and the tub would double for the Pacific Ocean. It was sunken a few feet and boiling with jetspa activity. Floating in the middle of this sea of bubbles was Joe Attanasio's head. Up close, I got a better look than I had that morning. He must have been close to ninety. His skin was like yellowing parchment and he was wearing this stupid coal-black Elvis wig with sideburns. One heavy lock fell down onto his wrinkled forehead. His eyes burned with a light that bordered on the unnatural. I would have laughed at the old fart if what I saw in his eyes didn't spook me.

"Donnie," he rasped. "Come here, man. Help me out. Let's have a look at this little gal."

The gorilla bent and lifted the old geezer like he was a kid. Attanasio came out of the bubbles buck naked, dripping wet, and totally disgusting. Not a sight for the weak hearted and I've always counted myself in that group. Being the coward I am, I turned away.

Some minor ruckus went on behind me. And then the old man began to laugh. I could tell he was hooked back up to his breather because what came out sounded like a combination of James Earl Jones and Elvis run through a vacuum hose. "Hey, doll. Turn around and have yourself a look at a real man."

Oh swell. Doesn't that just sound like the highlight of the evening? But I turned around anyway.

He was sitting in his wheelchair now, a black silk robe hanging on his scrawny old bod. There was a garish ring on every withered finger, and speaking of withered —

His pitiful legs and feet stuck out from under the robe, so thin they were barely there, the skin mottled and covered in ulcers. His twisted gray feet ended in long black toenails that hung over the front of his rubber bath shoes like talons. If this was a real man, I swore to be celibate for the rest of this life, and well into the next.

He put his glasses on, magnifying his unholy eyes to a point just beyond scary. I shuddered, but braced myself. I couldn't go back to Houston empty handed again. I had to learn what the old bastard knew.

Squinting, he croaked, "What the hell? They run out of good looking women over there at that worthless agency?"

Surely I hadn't heard right. "Excuse me?" Like I should care what this miserable asshole thought — but every girl has her pride.

"You got no tits, short hair, and you're too old to boot. Get the hell out."

Wait a minute. "Old? I'm old? What's it say on your birth certificate, Methuselah?"

He cackled. "Oooh, spunky. Hang on a minute. We might be able to work something out here after all. How are your enemas, Red?"

Enemas? Now I know I'm in the freakin' Twilight Zone. "Look, Mr. Attanasio. I'm not even from the agency. I have to admit I used this as a cover to get in. I'm not a nurse. I'm a writer. My current project is about a reporter named Houston Powers who disappeared around the time Don Bolles was murdered. An old associate of yours, Max Dunlap..."

I saw a flicker in his eyes — was it Houston? Or was it the mention of Max Dunlap that fanned those burning coals? Or, who knows, maybe it was the gas he just passed. Whew! Something must have crawled up inside him and died. Choking, I tried to continue, "...told me you might know something that would help me."

He throttled his chair forward and began to make slow circles around me. It took every ounce of self control to not make a run for it.

"So...," he sounded less like Elvis and more like the Dark Lord of Sith now. The metallic wheeze made chills run up and down my spine. "...even more moxie than I thought. You come here, bluff your way in. Ain't much to look at, but you are one feisty little thing. What do you think about that, Donnie? Think there's hope for her, after all?"

Donnie grunted. I couldn't tell if it was a "yes" grunt, or a "no" grunt.

"What would you do for me if I gave you something to use in your little book? Would you show me your tits?"

Of course, I would. When hell freezes over. "I don't think so."

"This is how the game is played, little lady. Elvis gives you something. You give something back to Elvis. You know, tit for tat?"

I'm outta here. "Look, geezer. I said, no tit. And you can forget about the tat, too."

He wheeled around and blocked the doorway. "You don't know what you're missing."

He threw back his robe. "Hail to the King, baby."

And there he was. Or should I say, wasn't. Dear God in heaven, how did I get myself into this?

Without another word, I squeezed between "the King" and the door jamb when he grabbed my arm and —

"Oh, shit!"

Out of the blue came an assault of unspeakable images: Joe Attanasio, a merchant of death ordering the brutal murders of countless illegal aliens and traitorous employees...

...and a sudden explosion blows apart a white Datsun leaving a shattered man writhing in pain on the blistering pavement.

I jerked away, unable to hold back the words. "You did it. You had Bolles murdered. It was you all along. And they never knew..."

His face darkened into a vicious twisted mask. "Who told you that?"

I shoved the chair real hard, sending it and the old man pell-mell across the slick tile to slam up against the tub. Joe flipped out of the chair and splashed down head-first. As his breathing tube filled with water, he did one hell of a sputtering imitation of Lloyd

Bridges in *Sea Hunt*. The Elvis wig swam off in search of other sea anemone.

Donnie lurched to haul the old man out.

And me? I ran.

Up one hall and down another I fled, but I got turned around and instead of heading for the front door ended up lost in the Elvis wing. I could hear Donnie huffing and puffing as he searched through room after room. I was faster than he was, but that wouldn't do me much good if he ever got his hands on me.

But finally there it was. I had the front door in sight and sprinted for it but came to a skidding stop when I heard the Darth Vader rattle and the hum of the electric wheelchair motor. He skidded around the corner on one wheel like a geriatric Mario Andretti and yelled: "Do you feel lucky, punk? Well, do ya?"

Holy mother of God. He had a gun. A really big gun. I threw up my hands, "Oh shoot."

He aimed right at my nose.

"No! Wait. Wait. It's just a figure of speech."

He fired....

Chapter Ten

I flung myself to the ground just as a bullet whizzed overhead and took out the chandelier. Shards of crystal fell like rain.

The kick of the gun propelled Joe back about ten feet or so and while he recovered, I scrabbled back through the open door behind me. I slammed it shut and locked it.

Wood splintered everywhere as bullets blasted through the door. Breathing hard, scared shitless, I looked for cover and voila! There it was. My salvation. Elvis' pink Cadillac convertible. I dived into the front seat and covered my head as bullets flew.

Donnie kicked open the door and Joe rolled in still firing that hand cannon. Round after round. The windshield shattered and I gotta tell you I thought I bought it for sure. I made a vow to go straight to the light. None of this haunting crap for me. No percentage in it.

And that's when I saw the keys. I reached over, turned the ignition, and the engine roared to life. Yes, Virginia, there is a Santa Claus. I threw it into reverse and pushed the gas pedal down with my hand.

Donnie threw himself on the hood as the tires smoked and squealed on the slick tile. The Caddy shot backward. Donnie went spinning off and wound up head-first in the marquee.

I only got one quick look but sparks were flying and I think Donnie's hair was on fire.

The marquee now read: Elvis Trouble.

The Caddy smashed right through the wall into the makeshift showroom, plowing under cocktail tables and patrons, then right up onto the stage as the motion sensor kicked in: *Hunka hunka burning love.*

I took out the fat Elvis with one of the tailfins. He flew into the air, did a triple somersault and landed face-down in the back seat. *I'm just a hunka hunka burning love.*

"Shut up!"

The second wall fell victim to the roaring Caddy, decapitating all those stupid dolls. Elvis heads ping-ponged everywhere.

The third wall came crashing down just like Joshua had blown his horn. There were gold records spinning around the room like demented Frisbees.

Hunka hunka hunka hunka.

I was screaming my head off, but somehow found the inner strength to keep that accelerator mashed all the way to the floor. Okay, so it wasn't exactly inner strength. Okay, so I was too freakin' scared to let go. You want to make something of it?

The fourth wall was a ten-foot glass patio slider. It shattered as we catapulted straight back, fins first, into the Olympic size pool.

I watched the Caddy and the fat Elvis go down for the count. *Hunka hunka gurgle gurgle.*

"Does this mean Elvis has left the building?"

I hauled myself out of the pool, and raced across the manicured lawns, around the front to my car. Do you know how hard it is to run in a wet skin-tight nurse's uniform?

I snatched the keys from my front pocket and started her up. Just as I was pulling out, I looked into the rearview mirror to see Attanasio rolling down the rose-lined walkway blasting away with that Dirty Harry special.

It boomed into the night. Blew the top off the mailbox. Beheaded the statue of a small boy peeing into a pool. Pruned a couple of trees. Not a single light went on in the neighborhood. Not a single person came out to see what all the ruckus was about. Guess they were used to it by now.

I was scared. Shaking. Barely able to steer the car. I should have called the police but who would they believe, him or me? After all, some crazy lady lies about who she is, forces her way into your home, then methodically destroys it — what would you do? Shoot the bitch.

All I wanted to do was hightail it for home. So that's what I did.

* * * * *

I stuffed my face all the way up I-17 — a Milky Way bar, a Snickers and two Yoo-Hoos.

I kept looking down at the cell phone lying on the console. The need to call my "ex" and beg for help was overpowering. Yes. It was the weenie thing to do, but I didn't care. I didn't give a damn if he was playing hide the salami with that blonde weasel. I just wanted someone to be there for me, and for such a long time he'd been the someone.

Before I knew it, he answered.

"Andrew? It's — ah — Matilda."

After a long silence, I heard, "What's wrong now?"

"Nothing," I lied. "I just wondered how you're doing." My voice quivered, dammit. I couldn't help it.

"You crying?" he asked in an irritated voice.

"No. Just allergies." Why shouldn't I be crying? My safe, sheltered little world was gone forever. I was adrift, without the tools I needed to survive. And someone shot at me! Bullets! Big bullets! Help me, Andrew! You always took care of me before. But instead I said, "How's Elizabeth?"

"You've got to get hold of yourself, woman. It's over. Try and be a big girl."

It was a barrel of iced Gatorade on top of my head. When I quit reeling from the shock, I came to my senses. "You're right, as usual, Andrew. Have a good life." I had to add, "Oh by the way, your money says 'hello'."

"Bitch." He hung up.

I felt so much better.

Just outside Sedona, I called and alerted Chloe I was coming by, had to get my dawg, you know. I needed Haggis' warm little body beside me for comfort. And besides, I figured he was probably having an asthma attack from the incense and sage that hung in her place like fog. The little guy was thrilled to see me if wet, slurpy kisses are any indication.

Then we hurried on home. It struck me that my haunted gingerbread house was now really and truly my home. My safe haven. My shelter from the storm. And my own personal all-night Studio 54, if I didn't get Houston out soon. But that was all about to change. I could hardly wait to liberate him. In short work, I'd solved the case. He was practically knocking on the pearly gates.

* * * * *

"I know who murdered you, Houston. It was Joseph Attanasio, the ex-mob kingpin. He made the call to have Bolles killed. To cover it up, when you started snooping around, he made you number one on his hit list. It's the logical explanation. Damn, I'm good." I was out of breath. "Don't you think?"

But Houston didn't see it that way. "Don't go putting away your gumshoes, Tildy. You haven't solved anything yet."

"What?" I stared back at his now familiar face behind my bathroom mirror. "Get out of there so I can brush my teeth."

He vanished and reappeared perched on the edge of the tub.

"I did solve it. Joe Attanasio killed you. I know it was him. I'm sure of it."

"Okay, let's just say I buy that. Show me your eyewitness. Your forensic evidence." He spoke patiently as if explaining things to a small child, "There's nothing to connect him to *my* murder. You're not finished."

"Oh yes, I am." I spit in the sink and wiped my mouth. "That asshole shot at me. I'm just a pampered housewife from Chicago." I hit the light switch and went into the bedroom. "No matter what they say about Chicago, we're not used to people shooting at us. I could wind up dead."

"You're right of course." Houston popped in ahead of me. "I don't know what I was thinking. It's not worth the risk."

I stopped dead in my tracks. "Did you just say I was right?"

Houston nodded and smiled amiably.

Uh-oh, I was in big trouble now. Dead or alive, this guy was smarter than I was. I knew it. He knew it.

I moved Haggis off my pillow and climbed into bed. "I'm glad you see it that way."

Houston jumped into bed beside me and tried to fluff his pillow but it wasn't working out. He kept sinking down until his head was all I could see. "Nighty-night, Tildy. Don't let the bedbugs..." It was like sleeping with Louis the Sixteenth.

"Get over it. I'm not changing my mind." I switched off the light, closed my eyes and waited. I knew better than to think this was the end of it. It wasn't.

"Tildy? You asleep?"

"Yes!" The adrenaline rush from my close encounter of the worst kind was gone and I was completely drained.

"I just want you to know, I understand."

"Big of you, since I'm the one dodging bullets," I grumped. "Go to sleep."

Not even a minute later. "Tildy?"

"Hmmm?"

"I can't sleep," he whined. "I'm too upset. Thinking about hanging around here for all eternity. Pointless existence. Nothing to do except..."

All around the room colored strobe lights began to flash. Houston leaped onto the foot of the bed and begin to spin and gyrate, as the Brothers Gibb warbled yet another disco ditty.

"...practice my dance moves."

I pulled the covers over my head.

"And now, ladies and gentlemen and doggies, let me introduce the one and only, the Dancing Queen, Tildy MacNamara."

A spotlight hit me as the harmonic sounds of Abba filled the room. It wouldn't have been too bad except Houston and Haggis were singing along in a different key. It was hopeless. I'd never get to sleep this way.

I threw off the covers and sat up. "Okay, you win."

The lights faded and the sudden silence was deafening. "What do you want me to do?"

"Go back to work. You need hard evidence. You have to start over."

I looked at him a long time. He was right of course, although I'd never admit it to him. Even Columbo couldn't make a case outta what I had. "Okay, I'll begin again. First thing tomorrow. You know what Mary Poppins always says..."

"Wait!" He held up his finger. "I know this one. Supercalifragilisticexpiallidocious?"

I dropped my head into my hands. "No. That's not what I meant. Mary Poppins says: 'Well begun is'..."

Chapter Eleven

"...half done?"

Chloe turned back at the door.

"God no. Well done. Don't go bringing me something still crawling around on the plate."

Chloe made a circle with her thumb and forefinger. "Gotcha, boss lady. Be right back." The door banged shut behind her.

My mouth was watering at the thought of one of Ellie Jean's wonderful burgers, I squatted down beside the "bestseller" table and finished unpacking Sylvia Browne's latest title on reincarnation. The bell over the door jangled. From my low point of view all I could see under the table was a pair of shiny black boots and khaki pants.

"Can I help you?"

A sexy, resonant male voice, music to my celibate ears, called out, "I'm looking for Matilda MacNamara."

"Well, you found her. What can I do...." The words froze in my throat as I stood up and found myself facing a broad chest with a badge. Shit! Attanasio beat me to the punch. He'd turned me in for wrecking his house, among other things.

As I looked up into the handsome face and dark penetrating eyes of a six-foot-four (if he was an inch) Indian, I gulped, the hard beat of *Chain Gang* already ringing in my ears. "I can explain everything, Officer."

He interrupted. "Wait a minute. My warrant says Matilda MacNamara is seventy-six. Gotta say you're holding up really well."

I sagged in relief. Okay, if you want to get picky about it, I nearly fell down. "My aunt. You're not after me. You're looking for my aunt. She died. We have the same name."

"Oh, sorry. I didn't know. She had some old speeding tickets." His eyes narrowed. "Why did you think I was looking for you?"

Okay, Tildy. Think fast. "Ah — no reason." Brilliant as always. He put out his hand. "Sheriff John Yazzie."

"You're John Yazzie?!" When we shook I had a sudden flash of Houston Powers angry and hurt in a way I'd never seen him. I jerked away and stepped back.

"Is there a problem, ma'am?"

"No. No," I stuttered. "Why do you ask?"

"You seem really nervous."

Get a grip Tildy. "Nervous? I'm not nervous. Too much caffeine. Always makes me like this."

"Maybe you should try the decaf." I noticed he spoke slowly and seemed to choose every word carefully. "What's your interest in Houston Powers?"

"Who? Powers? I don't think I know anybody with that name."

"Really? The Chief said you picked up a report on an old case of mine, involving the disappearance of a reporter named Houston Powers."

The vindictive little man snitched me out, all because of his rotten French poodle. I should have kept my mouth shut about the damn dog.

"Why is that a problem, Sheriff Yazzie?" The best defense is a good offense. "Aren't police reports a matter of public record?"

"Someone starts digging around in a twenty-five-year-old unsolved case, an officer of the law thinks maybe he's got a reason to ask questions."

"It's nothing really. I'm starting a newsletter for my customers with a series on mysterious and supernatural things that happen here. When I came across this Bolles deal on the Internet and how all these reporters were sent out to finish his investigation, it piqued my interest. I was looking for an angle for my newsletter. That's all. I've been doing a lot of research on it. Here. Phoenix." Excellent, Tildy. Part truth, part lie, makes it tough to ferret out which is which. "Powers' name came up in my research. That's all," then, "Did you know him?" Tildy, Ace Detective, always on the job.

His back went ramrod straight and I got the impression he was surprised, even if his stoic expression never changed. "Why would I know him? I was just the officer assigned to the case. That's all. I didn't know him personally or anything." His aura went from purple and blue to muddy brown.

Didn't know him, huh? Liar, liar, pants on fire.

The bell over the door jingled again as Chloe walked in and the smell of char-broiled cow filled the store.

"Hey, it's Sheriff John," Chloe called excitedly. "Wow. Did we get robbed?"

Yazzie looked almost relieved at the interruption. He touched the brim of his Stetson and nodded politely. "No, ma'am. Just a routine matter. Some really old speeding tickets."

"Good old leadfoot Matilda. You write 'em, she stuffs 'em in the glove box. Must have had twenty or so tickets jammed in there." Chloe set the lunch bag on the counter. "Looks like you're a day late and a dollar short, Sheriff."

"Story of my life, ma'am. Miss MacNamara here told me she died. I'll just be on my way."

His big legs carried him to the door. I noticed Chloe's mouth was hanging open, her eyes shining with admiration.

Sheriff John may have been nurturing a budding set of love handles, but he was still a helluva good-looking man.

"What a hottie!" Chloe breathed, then reached into the bag for our burgers.

I watched through the window as Sheriff John climbed into his Expedition. Yes, he was a fine specimen, no doubt about it. But after that vision, and his obvious jitters, I was pretty damn sure that if he didn't off Houston outright, he either had something to do with it, or knew who did. I grabbed a hot, salty fry and popped it into my mouth. "Yep," I said, "He's just a hunka hunka burnin' love."

Little did I know, I was right.

Chapter Twelve

"You were sleeping with John Yazzie?" I nearly choked on my chocolate cream pie.

Houston was choking too, only he was choking back excitement. "How is he? How'd he look? Is he still the sexiest man in the world? What's he been doing with himself? What'd he say? Did he mention me?"

I was as stuck as a scratched record. "You were sleeping with John Yazzie? But, but..." I sputtered. "...that means he's gay!?"

He took a deep breath and let it out. "That's what I like about you, Mac. Mind like a steel trap."

"Gay?" I was beside myself. "What a shame," I lamented. "Such a waste of prime male flesh."

That got a rise out of him. "And what am I? Dog meat? Sure. Make nasty cracks about the gay dead guy who can't defend himself."

"No. I just meant, he's so, so strapping."

"Yeah," he sighed dreamily. "He is. Isn't he?"

Lovers. Can you beat that? And Yazzie said he didn't even know Houston. Guess he did — in the Biblical way.

It suddenly hit me that I had to tell Houston his lover was probably the man who killed him. Swell. Another letdown for my thin-skinned (and I mean that literally) friend. I was beginning to wonder if there'd ever come a time when I'd have good news for the poor guy.

"Houston, sit down. I've got good news and I've got bad news. Which do you want first?"

"Oh, Christ, now what?" But he did sit down, if you can call that sitting.

"I know who murdered you."

He snorted. "Again?"

"Okay. I deserve that. Maybe I was wrong the first time." I jabbed my finger at him. "But this time I'm positive. I had an episode."

He yawned dramatically. "You sure it wasn't indigestion?"

"The culprit is John Yazzie."

Houston gaped at me, then laughed. "Oh, that's a good one. Next you'll be telling me it was J. Edgar Hoover."

"No, he's dead."

"Hoover's dead? Oh, my God. Since when?"

He wasn't making this any easier. "Just shut up and listen. I know it was John Yazzie. When I touched him, I got a flash of you and him fighting. He came to the store asking questions about you, nervous as hell. He denied even knowing you."

"Well, duh." At this point I could tell Houston thought I was a moron. "A gay Navajo cop in a redneck county like this? He'd be stupid not to be nervous."

My confidence was shaken, not stirred. "You don't think it was him?"

But maybe he did after all. He was obviously re-thinking it. I could tell by the troubled look on his face, that and the way he was fading in and out.

"You're beginning to believe it, too — that Yazzie went bad and somehow got himself in the Mafia's pocket. If he was in bed with Attanasio, how far would he go to protect that secret from getting out? Would he kill to keep it?"

There was sadness in his eyes. "No, Tildy. That's not it at all. John would never throw in with the likes of Attanasio. He's the pride of his nation, a man who loves being a Navajo and being a cop. Since he was a kid, John's father and his political cronies groomed him for sheriff. It was his whole life. It was his destiny. I'm wondering if I was a threat to that future." He looked up at me, and ghost tears filled his eyes. "I'm wondering if our affair was a secret worth killing for."

"Oh, Houston, I'm so sorry." My heart ached for him. "Did you love him?"

"I still do." And I could see that it was true. "I never met anyone like John before. You should have seen him, Tildy. He was like a god straight down from Olympus."

"Well," I had to admit, "he ain't bad now."

"He swept me off my feet. Poetry. Romantic picnics by the creek."

"Poetry? Yazzie?"

"Shakespeare. Love sonnets."

"Really?" I was flabbergasted.

"I have to tell you, Tildy. No one ever treated me like that. I was flattered."

"Flattered?"

"Well, wouldn't you be? I mean here's this beautiful man, who could have anyone in the whole wide world and he chooses me?"

"I don't want to rain on your parade, Houston, but how many gay men were there in this part of the country twenty-five years ago? Probably not growing on trees, you know what I mean?"

"You mean he was so desperate he hopped in the sack with a dog like me?"

"Take a chill pill, for crying out loud." God, he was so touchy. "Anybody would die to have you, Houston, homosexual, heterosexual, bisexual. You're a real stud muffin."

"Is that a compliment?" He sniffed.

"Hell, yeah. It is."

* * * * *

I don't know about you, but I was pissed. Anybody who'd selfishly use a sweet guy like Houston, then just as selfishly murder him needed to be tracked down and strung up. I promised myself Sheriff John wouldn't get away with it.

But how do you go about accusing the County Sheriff of murder? Especially when everybody seemed to think this guy was the second coming?

First, I talked to Chloe. And you've probably already guessed how that went.

"John Yazzie?" she sighed. "Well, you know. He's like some guy out of the movies. He's sexy, and he's so brave. Like that time he waded out in the flood with nothing but this flimsy lifeline just to save a drowning dog. He can park his Tony Lamas under my bed any time."

I just patted her hand. "I don't think so, honey. You're a little, uh, young for him."

And then, there was my old pal, the local Chief of Police, Bill Parrish. He was remarkably nice, considering our last encounter.

"John? Hell, I've known John for twenty years. You'd have to look far and wide to find a cop tougher on crime than John Yazzie. We all think the world of him. You can put that in your newsletter."

If this kept up, I was going to have to really do a bloody newsletter. No biggie, I'd just squeeze it in between running the bookstore, Republican Party soirees, visits to the State Prison, and demolishing gangsters' cribs.

"Well, thanks, Chief Parrish. That's exactly what I wanted to hear." Not.

I would have made a clean, quick getaway if hadn't been for that gimpy young cop I'd pissed off on my first visit. He came hobbling in on his crutches, mad as a hornet, demanding to know: "Who the hell parked in the handicapped spot without a permit?"

I smiled lamely as the Chief gave me the evil eye. When he handed me the ticket, he asked, "You wouldn't be in the market for a puppy, would you?"

My conversation went a lot smoother with Ellie Jean, who owned the café down the street from the bookstore.

"Sheriff John? Helluva guy. Ask any business owner. They'll tell you he's good for tourism. Hard on crime, easy on the eyes. Nobody like our Sheriff John. One in a million."

He was one in a million all right. A gay Navajo. It's a miracle he ever got elected.

Chapter Thirteen

I took the day off from books and crooks. All work and no play makes Tildy completely nuts. Grace and I had tickets for the Shakespeare Summer Festival production of *The Taming of the Shrew*. Sedona, it turns out, is a Mecca for the arts.

Grace lived above her shop in a huge open space converted into living quarters. The place was like Grace, warm and comfortable with a dash of Southwestern chic. She was waiting out front when I drove up.

Grace hopped in, looking sharp in a jade squaw blouse over a pair of soft khaki pants stuffed into knee-high nu-buck boots. "I could eat a horse, girl," she said with a growl. "Let's get going."

I put my foot to the pedal and moved out into traffic. "I'm ready-freddy. My name is Tildy MacNamara. I'm an enchiladaholic and it's been three days and fifteen minutes since I had one."

"I hear ya. I've got the shakes, too."

In a few minutes, we pulled into the parking lot of Casa Rincon. The place sits on the highway to Cottonwood. It's built to look like an old Mexican hacienda. It's not really Mexican and it's not a hacienda — but the margaritas and the salsa put up a pretty damn good argument.

I pulled down the vanity mirror and had a look. Houston, damn him, was right. Again. The new haircut I'd sprung for that afternoon was just what the doctor ordered. Perky yet sophisticated — and I swear I looked ten years younger. Honest to God.

Grace, as good-looking as she was, had nothing on me. I'd chosen a black Pima cotton western blouse. The yoke was accented with silver conchas fastened by red leather ties. My black jeans fit my firm-if-Buick-sized butt real nice. I'd gone with red leather thongs with big silver buckles to set off the ties. My period was a week away, so my skin was smooth and pimple-free with a little bit of left-over tan from my recent hellish trip to Phoenix. Lord, I hadn't looked this good since college.

We drank margaritas, stuffed ourselves on chips and salsa, drank some more margaritas and did some serious damage to the Number Six Enchilada Combo Platter. By the time they brought the fried ice cream and sopapaillas, I'd already unbuttoned my jeans.

It seemed as good a time as any to bring up a subject that had been bothering me for weeks. Contrary to popular urban legend, I'm not completely stupid. I know my psychic abilities aren't everything they should be. Sometimes I'm right on the money, and other times I crap out. "Screwy" is what Andrew used to say, "those screwy episodes."

But every time I touched Grace I got the same vision. I was convinced there was a fiery death in Grace's future. I'd never told her I'm psychic — in fact, most of the time, I'm not. I hadn't wanted to bring it up because I was afraid it would affect our friendship. I didn't have many friends and God knows I've driven off enough people over the years. But when you love somebody, you don't want to see them hurt. It was worth the risk, so I bolstered my courage with the rest of my drink and just blurted it out.

She listened politely, and I thought maybe I was getting through to her, then she drained her glass and breathed a deep sigh. "Tildy dear." I noticed she didn't touch me. "You're so sweet to worry. I'll stay far far away from all burning buildings. Really I will. But, honey, you don't really believe in all that crap. Do you?"

I just looked at her, then, "Waiter? Two more margaritas, please."

* * * * *

After our third margarita we were feeling no pain and giggling like schoolgirls. So, we had our cute little waiter, Eduardo, call a cab.

In less than ten minutes a pink minivan pulled up and guess who was behind the wheel.

"Oh my God! Look Grace, it's my old buddy Chief Parrish. How's it hangin', Chief?"

He gritted his teeth. "Where to?"

We crawled into the cab and sat on the floor.

Grace waved at him over the seat. "To the Cultural Park, Jeeves, and make it schnappy."

"Christ on a crutch," he groaned. "Get your asses up and fasten those seatbelts or we're not leaving this parking lot."

Grace couldn't seem to get her seatbelt fastened, partly because of that rascal Jose Cuervo, and partly because she was so busy flirting with the Chief. "I just love a forceful man."

I was all belted in and ready for warp speed when I remembered. "Oh my God. How's your poodle?"

The Chief stomped on the gas pedal, "Why me?" and we lurched out of the parking lot.

* * * * *

By the time our moonlighting Chief of Police dumped us in front of the Sedona Cultural Park, Grace and I had sobered up a little and could make it in under our own steam.

The Park was already packed. Who knew the Bard would have such a following in Sedona? The only table we could find was off to the side of the grassy seating area.

Lightning forked in the distance illuminating the red rocks. Chloe said the monsoons were early this year. So far the storms had missed us, but it was still a pretty fancy light show.

My chair was sitting lopsided in the grass and kinda wobbly. At least I thought it was the chair. After all those margaritas, it could have been me that was wobbly. But the rising wind was cool on my tequila-flushed cheeks, and my head was beginning to clear.

I noticed Sheriff John standing near the stage, just off to the side. He was wearing his best cop face and his piercing gaze swept the crowd. But you and I both know, he wasn't there on official business. The asshole was there to steal Will's material for his love arsenal. How many gullible young men had he taken advantage of and cast aside like so much trash? Were there others besides Houston whom he'd lured to his bed and then murdered in cold blood? All right. I tend to get a little dramatic when I've been drinking. But, geeze, every word was the gospel truth.

Grace followed my stare. "Ah, Sheriff John. A stone cold fox. Too bad he's a cop."

"What do you know about him?" I reached down and scratched my ankle.

"Not much. Why?"

The truth is always better than a lie. "I have a friend who's hot for his bod." Now I scratched behind my knee. And scratched.

And scratched. Or tried to anyway. It was kinda tough through the denim.

"Yeah? If you want the goods on Sheriff John, talk to Wade Johnson."

I began to squirm. Felt like something was crawling all over me. "Senator Wade Johnson? You know him?"

"Yeah, I used to date a friend of his. Ted Cochran."

I looked down and noticed that one leg of my teetering chair was sitting in the middle of an enormous ant hill. Yikes! I jumped up, kicked my chair back and began to stomp my feet. "Look out! Ants. Big ones."

Grace jumped up, too.

We both squinted at the ground, but the nasty little buggers blended with the grass and the night. "You never told me you dated Ted Cochran."

Grace squirmed and brushed her legs. "He's the big fish that got away."

All of a sudden the bastards started stinging and I started dancing. "But what does Wade Johnson have to do with Sheriff John?"

As she watched my gyrations with a worried look on her face, Grace said, "He's an old friend of Yazzie's dad. Known John since he was a kid." It was contagious, now she was swatting her legs nearly as frantically as I was. "What should I do?" she yelled. "Should I call 911?"

A sudden clap of thunder shook the amphitheater. A bolt of lightning crackled nearby and my hair stood on end. That's when the skies opened up and God put a serious damper on *The Taming of the Shrew*. I forgot about the ants in my pants, and bolted, along with everyone else, to the only dry spot in the whole place. The stage.

Hundreds of us were packed like sardines into the few square feet of the proscenium — all the actors, all the audience, and all my ants. I don't know about everyone else, but I could barely breathe. I kept getting elbowed in the boobs and kneed in the butt. That's when, "YEOW!"

The ants began to seriously chow down on my ass. There was nothing I could do except...

"Oh my God," a shrill voice cried. "She's taking off her clothes!"

It was like the parting of the Red Sea. Standing there in my white cotton underwear, I suddenly had more elbow room than I would ever need.

Someone tapped me on the shoulder.

I turned around and found myself staring into the craggy but still-handsome face of Wade Johnson, the Senate Majority Leader. He held my ant-covered jeans gingerly by two fingers. "May I?"

In between scratching the welts on my legs and bottom, I started to laugh. "By all means..." You have to admit the whole deal was pretty absurd. "...get 'em."

He threw down my ant-ridden pants with a flourish, put his hands on his hips and began to do a mean Mexican hat dance on top of them.

The crowd broke into applause.

The Senator smiled at me.

I smiled back.

"You go girl," Grace whispered in my ear. "I think he likes you. You're the only person I know who can act like a total blithering idiot and be cute at the same time. How do you do it?"

God only knows. But the good-looking-for-an-older-guy Senator was definitely making goo-goo eyes in my direction. Was Grace right? Did he like me? Or was it just gas?

I flashed back to the photographs in Evelyn Johnson's den and my mind's eye began to connect the dots: Johnson, Cochran, Attanasio. Shit. Was he here because of my catastrophic visit to the Mafia mansion?

It could just be a coincidence. It could be I'm paranoid.

It could be I was making a mountain out of...

Chapter Fourteen

"...an ant hill!" Chloe burst into laughter as she finished reading the article which was (I can't believe I'm telling you this) on the front page of the freakin' *Sedona Red Rock News* the very next morning. Complete with color photos of me in my undies! Why oh why don't I wear pretty silk panties like the rest of the female population?

I glared at Chloe and said frostily, "You know, it's a sorry day when you make fun of a friend's misfortune. Especially when that friend is also your boss."

She had no shame. Her hysterical laughter was completely out of control. The fool.

The bell over the door jingled and I turned toward what I hoped would be a chance to forget about my humiliating experience at the Shakespeare Festival. But no such luck.

Joaquin sailed in like some Norse god. He was carrying a big cardboard box. If the printing on the outside was any indication, the devastatingly good-looking son of a bitch had brought me a case of Raid Ant and Roach Killer. It was going to be a long day.

Ellie Jean made it a point to personally bring our lunch over — wrapped in a copy of the damn newspaper, of course. And Grace dropped by with a bag of chocolate-covered ants — cute, real cute.

Even Bill Parrish got into the act, stopping by to razz me about autographing a copy of the photograph. Said he was thinking about having it framed and hung in the lobby, along with copies of all my citations.

I took the whole thing like a champ, if I do say so myself. I mean, after all, not one of them so much as even asked how my poor welt-covered bottom was. And there I was painted in Calamine lotion and drugged out on Advil — BUT — we sold more books that day than we had the whole week before. Guess celebrity has its perks — or should I say notoriety?

About two in the afternoon, Wade Johnson walked in. Could you just die?

But, get this — he didn't come to make fun of me. He came bearing a bouquet of white roses. He smiled as he handed them to me, "To match your undies, my dear."

Straight to my heart — utterly charming.

Haggis liked him too. He kept trying to hump the Senator's leg. I shrieked and grabbed the little guy. "Chloe!? Help!"

She came rushing out from behind the counter, took Haggis from me, "Sorry about that, Senator." and carried him to the back room.

"Guess he figures screwing a Congressman's a good way to get into the news, eh?" Wade laughed. "Since your little friend there has already gone and broke the ice, how about a bite of supper at my cabin up in the hills tomorrow night? Nothing fancy. Grill a couple of steaks. Watch the moon come up." He looked after Haggis. "Just you and me, if you don't mind."

I was completely flattered and more than a little flustered "Oh. What time should I pick you up?"

His white teeth flashed in an engaging smile. "I'm the old-fashioned kind, Matilda. How about if I pick you up?"

Way to go, girl. Nothing like playing hard to get.

"About seven, then, Senator?" I asked.

"Call me Wade. I insist."

He was a confident man who used his power and position to his best advantage. But on him, it looked good.

Hallelujah! A date. It had been a long, dry spell, but I could see showers on the horizon. "See you at seven." I tried not to drool. "Wade."

* * * * *

We closed late that night. I betcha every man, woman and child in Sedona had come in for a look at me. I finally had Chloe and Joaquin circle them like sheep and herd them out the door at nine-thirty.

On the verge of starvation, I made a quick stop at the Burger King for a chicken sandwich and a chocolate shake. Traffic was non-existent that time of night and I made it home in about ten minutes.

I'd left the TV on for Houston and Haggis. CNN. He couldn't believe there was a twenty-four hour news channel and was addicted — Houston, not Haggis. Haggis preferred the Cartoon Network, specifically Scooby-Doo. One Scooby snack? Two? Three? Uh-huh. Uh-huh. Yes, it's true. I'm a cartoon freak myself. All good detectives get wrapped up in those spooky mysteries — helps us hone our craft.

Houston was glued to the set, fascinated by the week's latest Washington sex scandal. Like the rest of the free world, I didn't even bother to listen anymore. As far as I was concerned, they were all amateurs next to Clinton.

"Hi," I walked through to the kitchen and unpacked the Burger King bag.

Houston didn't even look up.

Between bites, I tossed out, "Hey! Come here."

"Hmm?" He floated in, but his attention was still on the boob-tube.

I snapped my fingers. "Yo. Listen up. I plan on doing some serious name-dropping here and I want your full attention."

"Okay." He came up through the middle of the table. "I'm all yours."

"I've got a date."

"That's it? You've got a date? That's your big news? Well, good. You need to get out more."

"With Senator Wade Johnson."

That got his attention. "What?" He squirted around the room like a deflating balloon. "Wade Johnson? Are you crazy? Or stupid? Or just desperate to get laid?"

Stupid? Desperate to get laid? "Wait a minute. Aren't you the one who was ragging on me to go get some evidence?" Was he worried? Or just bitchy? "Maybe that was some other dead guy I'm risking my neck to help."

He stopped ricocheting off the walls and calmed down a little, but he was still hanging out near the ceiling.

"Why shouldn't I go out with him?" I was getting a crick in my neck trying to talk to him.

"Johnson is in cahoots with Ted Cochran. And it's a short leap from Cochran to Attanasio." He floated lower. "Don't do it, Tildy. You haven't thought this through. You don't know what you'll come up against with this guy."

I gave the last bite of chicken to Haggis. He deserved it, since he'd been waiting for it with the patience of Job. "I have thought it through. Just because Wade is Cochran's friend doesn't mean he's a Mafia puppet. This man is the Senate Majority Leader for crying out loud. Think about that. He's not some common criminal. Houston, you can't believe all that stuff you see on TV."

"But it's the *news.*"

"Exactly." I could tell he didn't get it. After all, he was from another time when the news wasn't scripted, it happened. "Besides, Houston, I really like him. I want to go out with him. I haven't had a date since I was a sophomore in college."

He pounced. "Ah-ha. Just like I thought. Horny."

I threw up my hands, went upstairs, and turned on the shower.

My shadow — always there, always a pain in the neck was waiting. "I've got a bad feeling about this," he worried.

I turned and looked at him. "It'll be okay, Houston." Geez, what a nervous Nelly. "It's just dinner. No sweat."

Chapter Fifteen

"You think it's hot in here?"

"Not really, my dear. Maybe if you took off that scarf, or the jacket, or the vest." Wade smiled knowingly. "After all, it is June."

Guess my first-date jitters were showing. "I thought it might get chilly."

"I'll keep you warm, Mattie."

Who the hell's Mattie?

Yes. I was wearing a scarf and a jacket and a vest. Yes, I'm ridiculous. That's what came of listening to that haute couture dropout Houston. He said if Wade jumped my bones, all those layers would make it harder for him to "peel the onion" so to speak. I went along for two reasons: One — to placate Houston. And two — what if he was right?

As I stared out the limo window, sweat puddling in my bra, I came to two conclusions. One: Houston was a complete nutcase. And two: Houston was a complete nutcase. I took off the jacket.

I wasn't kidding when I said it had been over twenty years since my last date (if you don't count Andrew, and who in their right mind would?). Consequently, I didn't have the first clue how to act, what to say, or what to do.

"Have some champagne, Mattie." Wade patted my hand patronizingly "It'll settle you down."

Settle me down? Who did he think he was — my husband or something? I gritted my teeth, "Why not?" took the glass, chugged it and shoved it back at him. "Thanks."

I'm such a slow study. You'd think I'd have learned about ambitious assholes the first time around? This guy was Andrew the Anus twenty-five years from now.

Let's face it. I wasn't having a good time and prospects were getting dimmer by the second. So, the dating game dismally behind me, I was back to square one: get the goods on John Yazzie.

*   *   *   *   *

Wade's "cabin up in the hills" was more like a hotel than most hotels I've stayed at, an enormous two-story, eight-bedroom, five-bath lodge nestled among the cedars, surrounded by waterfalls and ponds. *Architectural Digest* cover material.

The "bite of supper" was five courses beginning with this monster Caesar salad tossed right at the table with home-made dressing, anchovies, the whole caboodle. The entree was cut-it-with-a-fork tenderloin grilled to perfection with melt-in-your-mouth creamed spinach; julienne potatoes as sidekicks. Belvedere vodka martinis were followed by three wine offerings and to top it all off, crême brulee — all served in the massive Ponderosa-style dining room by Wade's personal chef, an odd-looking man introduced as Chung Lee Hernandez. A guy with a name like that had to be a great cook.

After dinner, we danced to Tony Bennett on the terrace beneath a million stars, while Wade sang along. It was a catastrophe. You've heard the expression "tone deaf?" I think it was Wade's middle name. Ah yes, romance — and "sarcasm" is mine.

While we were leaving our hearts in San Francisco, Chung Lee wheeled out a bar cart, asking, "Will there be anything else, Senator?"

Wade dipped me (my back cracked and I knew there'd be hell to pay in the morning), then he said, "That's all for tonight, Chung Lee. The lady and I want to be alone."

Alone? Did he say alone? Chung Lee Hernandez turned to leave and...

"No. Wait!" Wade gave me a funny look, but didn't drop me. Thank God. "I need a drink."

As Chung Lee brought the cart over, Wade reluctantly let me up so I could browse.

"Oh," I mused. "Green Chartreuse." Maybe that would loosen up the old fart's tongue so I could find out what I needed to know and get the hell outta there. "Let's have some."

"Ah," he grimaced. "Not much use for it. My ex-wife liked it."

I batted my eyes. That works for some women, but I probably just looked like a fool with something stuck in my eye. "Oh come on, Wadesy. You know what they say about green Chartreuse?"

I could tell by his puzzled look he didn't.

"They say it's an eye opener. Fly opener." I leaned closer and whispered into his ear, "Thigh opener."

That got his attention. "Chung Lee, two. Straight up."

I knew it, lecherous scum bucket.

* * * * *

We were leaning against the terrace railing looking up at the stars when Wade said off-handedly, "I had you checked out."

I turned and looked at him, not knowing what to expect.

He emptied his second drink, "What can I say? I'm a man in the spotlight, can't be too careful." He went to the cart and poured us each a third. "You know, this stuff ain't half bad."

Did I detect a slight slur there, or was it just wishful thinking?

"My sources told me some pretty interesting stuff about you."

While he wasn't looking, I tipped my glass over the balcony. That's when I realized I had been dumping my drinks on his Range Rover.

"What interesting stuff is that?" Please don't say: Joe Attanasio wants you bumped off.

Wade drained his glass and went back for a refill. I'd created a monster. "They say you're psychic."

"Really? Who's 'they'?"

He closed his eyes and put his fingertips against his temples. "Tell me what I'm thinking."

It didn't take a psychic to figure that one out. "You're wondering how much longer before you get me in the sack."

I tossed another drink and watched it splatter on the car below. Yep. The Chartreuse was melting Wade's hood *and* his brain.

"Amazing," he uttered. "I could feel you in my head, baby." He drained his fifth drink. "Sssweetheart, I think that psssychic ssstuff isss sssexy asss ssshit."

"Sssexy? Easy for you to say."

Wade put his hand on my boob. That's all — just put it there, then spaced out. I moved his hand away and snapped my fingers in front of his face. "Wade? You in there?"

He repeated, "Sssexy."

Okey-dokey. I mentally rubbed my hands together in glee. Time for twenty questions. "My friend Grace tells me you know John Yazzie."

He smiled happily. "You mean Little John?" He held his hand about six inches over his head. "Why I've known Little John sssince he wasss just a whipper ssschnaper eatin' dirt on the reservation."

Eating dirt? That one got me.

"Me and Big John go way back to when we was workin' that ssscam with Ted. Had to get that Indian land."

I couldn't believe it. I got the scoop! And straight from the horse's mouth! Houston would be so proud. In my excitement, I dropped the shot glass over the edge of the balcony. It hit the windshield with a resounding pop. Cracks spread in every direction.

Wade and I looked down at the windshield. "Bummer." He put his arm around my shoulder. "Look at that."

"I'm really sorry, Wade."

"That's okay, sssugar." Without so much as a by-your-leave, he grabbed my hips, thrust his erection against me, "Ssshit happens," planted his hot wet lips over mine, and went into his toilet-plunger routine.

Did I ever tell you how much I like a firm-lipped kisser? Well, the Senator's lips were loose and slippery as raw liver.

Ah, romance.

I turned my head and felt the slobber run down my chin.

"Wade. Let go."

He didn't.

And the little voice inside my head said, "No problem, Tildy. You can take the old geezer in a New York minute."

That was when "the old geezer" swept me into his arms, carried me up the stairs and dropped me on his massive bed. He wasn't even out of breath. Old geezer, huh?

I slid to the edge, "Wade, think about how this will look on the front page of the *National Enquirer*."

He staggered over and locked the door with a key. "Nobody gonna know 'cept you and me. I won't tell if you won't."

When a man's that drunk you don't know whether a remark like that's a threat or a promise.

Then, to my horror, the good Senator picked up a remote and Patty LaBelle belted out: *Hey sister, go sister, soul sister, go sister,* as

Wade peeled off his shirt, revealing way too much muscle tone for a man his age. Eye-opener.

Getcha getcha ya-ya da-da. Wade unzipped his fly. Oh my God, fly-opener.

Getcha getcha ya-ya here. His slacks slid to his ankles. He stepped out of them and kicked them across the room to land smack on my face.

Ah, romance.

Mocha chocolata ya-ya. Creole Lady Marmalade.

And there he stood, in his socks and a pair of skin tight stars-and-stripes bikinis. I nearly saluted. What a bod for such an old fart. That's when I noticed Little Wade was saluting — yes, folks, a living testimonial to Viagra.

He pranced over to the bed, bumping and grinding.

I scooted as far back as I could, while he grinned and dropped the key down his shorts.

"Hey Mattie, voulez-vous coucher avec moi, ce soir?"

"Not tonight, dear. I have a headache."

His eyes rolled back and without so much as a "timber!" he fell face down on my crotch — thigh-opener — and passed out. I rolled him off and sat up, staring in dismay at the variety of geography in his bikinis. Among other things, I could make out the door key.

Now all I had to do was, oh lord in heaven, fish it out of his drawers.

Hello, hey Joe, you wanna give it a go?

I shoved my hand in among the skin folds and prickly hairs until my fingers closed over cool metal.

Getcha getch ya-ya da-da.

Wade raised his head and groaned, "Ohhh baby. You got the touch."

"Oh shut up." I shoved his head back down.

The fool was in ecstasy. He nearly sang, " That's it baby, give it to me rough. Attanasio must be nuts to want to bump you off."

EEEK! Joe Attanasio?

My blood ran cold. "I told you not to say that!"

My inner voice screamed, "Run, stupid! Get the flock out of here!"

I fumbled with the lock. Was it my imagination or was the key a little moist? Geez, Louise. I dropped it on the carpet, wiped my hands on my skirt, boogied down the steps and straight out the front door.

Houston had been right. Dead right — forgive the pun. Not only was Wade tied to Attanasio — he was his goddamn errand boy. I was in big trouble.

I dashed madly down the driveway to the bottom of the hill, tripping and stumbling, even falling a couple of times. My palms were scraped. My skirt was ripped and one knee was bloody. If it hadn't been for my boots, I probably would have broken my ankle.

Nearby, something snapped. I whirled around. What was that? "Who's there?" Nothing. Not a sound. "Is someone there?"

Something moved in the shadows, but I didn't wait around to see who or what it was. I took off like my ass was on fire and ran all the way to the main road and stopped. Wheezing like an old lady, holding the stitch in my side with one hand, I fumbled in my bag for my cell phone.

That's when a blinding spotlight caught me dead in the face.

I shrieked and threw up my hands.

"Don't shoot!"

One step back and the ground went out from under me. I rolled down into the muddy bottom of a shallow ditch and just lay there — the words: *All right, fine. Just come and get me, bastard,* running through my exhausted brain. I know what you're thinking: Why didn't you get up and run? But you weren't there. You weren't tired and scared. Every bone in your body wasn't aching. You weren't drunk as a skunk on Chartreuse.

The next thing I knew a flashlight was shining in my face and the resonant voice of John Yazzie was asking, "Miss MacNamara? Is that you down there? You need a hand?"

"I need two, if you don't mind."

He hauled me up and helped me into his car. Yes. He was the enemy, and he could have shot me right there on the spot. But he didn't.

As he drove me home, he only asked one question. "What were you doing in the ditch?"

And I only had one answer. "I was on a date."

After the night's fiasco I knew one thing for sure...

Chapter Sixteen

The dating game was definitely not my sport.

I sat on the tufted stool in front of my dressing table, "You know, Houston," picking gravel out of my stinging palms, "I really don't get what you see in men."

Houston watched from the edge of the tub, wincing, as I dabbed alcohol on my poor knee.

"Ow!"

"Oh, ow!"

"OH! OW! OW!"

"Crybaby. Stop whining," Houston said in disgust.

"It hurts."

Haggis joined in, whimpering and carrying on like he was the one with the severed limb, not me. Okay, so it wasn't a severed limb. It was just a scabby knee — it hurt. A lot. Damn it.

Haggis kept licking off the ointment.

"No, no, honey. It's the Mommy's outside medicine, not the Doggy's inside medicine." I pushed him gently aside, hissing as I dabbed on more ointment.

Houston folded his arms over his chest. "Did I tell you? Huh?" He could be a smug bastard when he set his mind to it. "What did I tell you? Did I tell you to stay home?"

"Okay. Fine. You told me." I put a Scooby Band-Aid on my knee, picked up my dog and limped into the bedroom.

Houston followed, still nagging: yada-yada, blah, blah, blah. It was going to be another one of those nights.

"When are you ever going to listen to me?"

PMS and exhaustion kicked in and I turned on him. "Just shut up. Would you?"

You'd have thought I slapped his face. "Well," he put his hands on his hips and his nose in the air. "Fine."

And he was gone — just your standard, run-of-the-mill, puff-of-smoke disappearance.

I looked around — in the closet, under the bed, behind the dresser. Yep. He was gone all right. If I'd known it was that simple, I'd have told him to shut up weeks ago.

I folded the quilt and laid it at the foot of the bed. Lights out, pillow fluffed, I sunk down into my featherbed and drifted off into dreamland.

Beside me, Haggis snored softly in my ear.

Ah, romance.

*****

Haggis' low growl reached down and jerked me out of a sound sleep. He landed on my chest with a thump, barking ferociously.

My eyes flew open.

"What? What is it?"

Something huge moved in the doorway. A jolt of panic clenched my stomach. Oh my God. Somebody was in the house!

A man.

A big man.

A really big man.

A really big flesh-and-blood man.

Adrenaline flooded into me. I grabbed a big book off the night stand and hurled it across the room. It found its target with a satisfying thump. Thank God for Thomas Wolfe and his tomes.

I hit the floor and snatched the bat from under my bed as strong fingers closed on my shoulder. I spun around and cracked him across the knee with the bat.

"Bitch!"

All it did was piss him off. He hauled me up and shook me until my teeth rattled. I couldn't hang onto the bat. It clattered to the floor and rolled under the bed.

Haggis came flying straight into his face, latched onto one ear and hung there.

The beast roared in pain and twisted madly until Haggis let go and flew onto the bed.

I sunk my teeth into one big hairy forearm and I *didn't* let go. My little highland warrior came back for another serving of the guy's earlobe.

The thug held me down with one hand and reached up with the other to tear Haggis away and toss him into the hall. I heard him hit the opposite wall and yelp.

Please don't let him be hurt.

I bit down harder and brought my knee up, aiming for his groin, but it was too little, too late. His fist smashed into my face and I saw stars for a split second. And then I didn't see anything else.

* * * * *

The next thing I knew, I was lying on the bedroom floor, vaguely aware of the sound of running water.

I groaned and squinted against the light coming from the bathroom. The big man was moving around.

What was he doing in there? Who was it? Wait. I'd seen him before. Then he turned and I got a really good look at the asshole.

Donnie the Gorilla! Attanasio's goon.

Jesus Christ. They'd really come for me.

He lumbered back in and I scooted under the bed.

"Aw, shit. Get outta there." He squatted down, grabbed my ankle and pulled me out. There was nothing I could do about it.

He dragged me across the floor toward the bathroom. I grabbed the bedpost and tried to hold on, but he jerked and my arm nearly came out of the socket.

"What do you want?" I screamed at him. Stupid question. I knew what he wanted.

"You're gonna take a little bath is all."

"Let go of me, asshole!"

I twisted and kicked and squirmed and fought with all my might. But it was no use. He picked me up, dumped me in the tub like a load of laundry, shoved me under and held my head down.

Water filled my nose and mouth; and panic filled my soul. I clawed at his hands. My oxygen starved lungs began to burn. The urge to take a deep breath was nearly irresistible. But I held it. I didn't want to die. Not now. Not like this. Hell, I was just getting a life.

It pissed me off. This son of a bitch wasn't going to win. Righteous anger boiled up and gave me a surge of strength. My flailing hand found my razor on the edge of the tub. And, baby, you better believe I knew what to do with it.

I slashed back with everything I could muster up. I didn't know what I'd hit, if anything, but I must have got something. He let go and bellowed.

I burst out of the water, sucking blessed air into my fiery lungs.

Donnie staggered back, holding his bloody face and screaming. "You cut me. You fucking bitch." He lunged for me again. And I swear I saw death in his eyes.

Haggis hit him from behind like a guided missile and latched onto his big, fat ass while I fought the tub, the water and the monster for all I was worth.

Donnie let go again and grabbed his butt. "What the...?"

I latched onto the rounded edge of the tub and slung one leg up over the side, just in time to see...

..."Jesus, Mary and Joseph!" Donnie careening across the room, slipping and sliding on the water slick tiles, Haggis hanging off his caboose. That's when I saw, of all things, my toilet brush wailing the bejeezus out of him.

For some reason I couldn't see him, but I knew the knight who wielded the brush. Sir Houston! My hero.

Houston, the Fuller Brush Man, was all over Donnie. Beating him on the head. Poking him in the eye and the throat. Haggis ran around and bit him in the kneecap, then started jumping up and down to make sure I was okay.

The brush was going to town. "What is it? Jesus! What is it?" Donnie shrieked.

The toilet brush connected with a jab to the solar plexus.

Donnie countered with an elbow to the bristles.

The brush blocked and delivered a devastating uppercut to the chin.

Donnie was hurt.

The brush moved in for the kill, landing a powerhouse punch to the head.

He's up. He's down. He's up again.

Donnie went down and stayed down. And he was screaming like a girl.

"Ow! Shit! Stop that! Help me! Jesus. Help."

He was scared out of his ever-loving mind. And it warmed the cockles of my heart.

The brush, like some bizarre cartoon character gone insane, was everywhere — dancing around the room, whipping this way and that way.

I hauled myself out of the tub, deciding to join the festivities. "Oh my God. It's a ghost. The brush is haunted!" I picked up the plunger and whacked him with it. "Run for your life!"

Donnie got up, shielding his head and face, and he ran, ladies and gentlemen. I'm here to tell you, he had some moves for such a big dude.

The toilet brush and I chased him out into the hallway. He tripped on the top step. I watched over the bannister as he thumped and bounced and banged and slammed and cursed all the way down. *Oh, that's gotta hurt.*

He landed with a resounding thud, curled into a ball and began to cry like a baby. The toilet brush kept smacking him on top of the head again and again and again — until Donnie was driven out the front door on his hands and knees.

My own knees were threatening to buckle. But I fought it off and somehow managed to get downstairs, Haggis right on my heels.

I looked around for Houston, but he and his weapon of choice were long gone. I cautiously stuck my head out the door and got a glimpse of Donnie hightailing it down the drive with the brush in hot pursuit. Haggis barked indignantly, but had no intention in joining the chase.

I slammed the door and locked it, for all the good it did. Attanasio's goon had broken out the stained glass panel and if he decided to come back...

...gulp.

I picked up the phone and dialed 911.

The Operator answered on the second ring,. "Nine-one-one emergency. What's your emergency?"

I was draining adrenaline faster than a cold pint on a hot day. My voice was a wreck. The bastard had nearly choked the life out of me — I'd coughed water until my throat was raw — and now, the hysteria I was barely keeping at bay combined to make my voice a hoarse whisper. "I was just attacked by a three-hundred pound gorilla."

"Excuse me? You were attacked by a gorilla?"

"He tried to drown me in my own tub. The one I ordered all the way from Phoenix. Can you believe that?"

The Emergency Operator wasn't impressed with my imported bath tub. "Did you consume any alcohol tonight?"

"Yes." A slug of Chartreuse would have hit the spot just then. "But not nearly enough."

She couldn't hide the suspicion in her voice. "Are you on any heavy medication?"

Chapter Seventeen

"I wish to God I was."

The young officer who'd shown up not more than five minutes after I called 911 glanced down at his notes in confusion. "Hmm. So you *weren't* armed?"

I shook my head. That was the third time he'd asked. "No. Not unless you count..."

"...the toilet plunger." He squinted at his notepad some more. "I see." It was pretty obvious, he didn't get it.

I wasn't sure I did.

Chief Parrish and two more squad cars showed up about that time and the old homestead was suddenly crawling with cops.

I could tell by the look on Bill's face he was genuinely worried about me, and that all the bluster and sarcasm camouflaged his real concern.

Like when he said with a perfectly straight face, "Can you describe this gorilla? Could you pick him out of a lineup with other gorillas?"

See what I mean?

"Oh, sure." I said bravely, trying to keep the quiver out of my voice. "You're making fun of me. Right?"

"Why no, ma'am. I wouldn't do that." Bill smiled gently. "Just tell me everything and keep it shorter than usual. I have a dentist's appointment next Tuesday."

"Cute."

"Yeah, but..." he waggled his heavy eyebrows, "...not as cute as you in that outfit."

I looked down, and, yeah boy, my nipples stood out like gumdrops against my soaked "PMS" tee-shirt. The heat rose in my cheeks and I quickly crossed my arms. Oh well, it took my mind off the self-pity.

"Tell me what happened." He at least had the decency to look me in the eye.

So, I explained everything from start to finish, omitting any mention of Houston and the attack of the killer toilet brush, but including (about damn time, you say) the story of my adventure at Joe Attanasio's house the week before.

"Psychic flash?" He repeated after I had finished. I knew he'd get stuck on that. "What the hell is a 'psychic flash'? And do you really expect me to arrest someone because you had one about the Bolles murder?"

"No, Chief. I don't expect you to go running down to Phoenix and slap the cuffs on the old don just on my say-so. I know you can't do that. Besides, it's not about that. It's about the goon breaking into my house tonight. It's about this." I pointed to my swollen and discolored face and neck.

The crime scene guy came downstairs carrying a silver metal case. "Got some nice blood samples, Chief. DNA match should be a breeze."

"See?" The Chief patted me on the back. "We're taking this seriously. Already got an all-points out on your gorilla. We'll send Phoenix P.D. over to Attanasio's place. The whole shebang."

My resentment toward him subsided when he said, "Sergeant Monroe, see if you can find some plastic sheeting to put over the door and make sure somebody keeps an eye on her."

It was beginning to look like Chief Parrish was a nice guy after all.

But when he and the CSI officer started to leave, he had to go and ask, "You check the medicine cabinet, Slocum? Any hallucinogenic drugs in there?" He said it loud enough to be sure I heard.

"No, sir." Slocum was surprised. "I didn't know I was supposed to check, sir."

As the door shut behind them, I yelled, "You should have checked under the mattress. That's where I keep my stash."

Forget the "nice guy" remark.

* * * * *

The sky was just getting light when Haggis began to whine.

"What is it, boy? You need to go out?" I reached over to scratch his ear, but instead stuck my hand in a cold, tingly puddle. I squinted, barely able to make out the someone or something lying next to me.

Then, "Shit!" I tumbled out of bed. A ghoul! It was the most awful thing I'd ever seen.

"It's only me, Tildy. Don't be scared." His voice was shrill and piercing as the wail of a banshee, yet weak as a kitten. It sent a chill all the way to my bones.

Houston looked absolutely terrible, even for a ghost. I identified him only by his black silk shirt and polyester bellbottoms. He was more corpse-like than I'd ever seen him. The pall of decaying flesh hung about the room. What happened to my handsome disco king?

His transparency had me worried, and more than a little frightened. "What the hell, Houston? What happened?"

"The manifestation, " he croaked.

"The what?"

"I connected to your world." He could barely speak. "Connected physically. It's the only way I could save you. It nearly, you'll pardon the expression, killed me."

Poor baby. I wanted to help him, or at least comfort him, but I couldn't even bring myself to look at him. "What should I do? This is all my fault. You saved me and now, just, oh God, look at you."

He laughed, kind of, or coughed. I wasn't sure which. "Is that a slam?"

"Will you be okay?"

"I don't know. This never happened before. I think I just need to recharge my batteries. Maybe if I could just lie here..."

Being extra careful not to come anywhere close to touching the poor miserable mess, I picked up my pillow and snagged my quilt off the foot of the bed, "I'll just leave you alone to rest, sweetie. If you need anything..."

He turned his normally expressive eyes toward me, and in the gray dawn light I could see they'd turned into bottomless obsidian pits. Traces of a rotting skull showed behind them. "No, Tildy. Stay with me. Please."

"Really?" I swallowed hard and tried to convince myself that looks aren't everything. This was Houston, my friend. I backed up and slowly eased into the rocker. Haggis jumped in my lap, still whining, still worried about our friend. And I'd say he had good reason. Wouldn't you?

"I won't leave, Houston. I'll be right here as long as you need me."

I put the pillow behind my head and wrapped the quilt around both Haggis and me. The musty dead smell in the room was nearly overpowering, but I'd laundered the quilt a couple of days before and the Downy kinda offset it.

I tried to go back to sleep, but every time I closed my eyes, a thousand and one images began to dance in my brain. Car bombs. Geriatric criminals in wheelchairs, with Elvis wigs. Men behind bars. Three-hundred pound gorillas. And friends with, shall we say, really bad skin.

I gave up after about half an hour and sat there, watching Houston return to "normal" inch-by-inch-by-inch.

At eight-thirty, I went downstairs and called for an appointment to get my front door fixed, have a security system installed, and my entire house fumigated.

I also called Joaquin and asked him to work my shift, then I went back upstairs and sat with Houston.

By noon, he was looking more like his old self.

When he was feeling better, he finally validated my theory that Attanasio was the prime mover behind the Bolles incident. And gosh, all I had to do was nearly die before he'd admit it. But it did my heart and my ego a world of good anyway.

While I was downstairs fixing a sandwich, the phone rang. It was my old bud, Chief Parrish with the good news that the gorilla was still at large (big surprise) — that Attanasio denied ever knowing the guy (big surprise) — that they wouldn't give up the search until they caught him and would maintain "surveillance" on the house (and that *was* a big surprise).

He thought I'd gone completely wacko when I asked him to check for Donnie at Wade Johnson's place. "Wade Johnson's. Why?"

He made a nasty crack about my "psycho" flash, so I let it go since I didn't really have a valid reason to send him out there.

That was the problem with the entire investigation. Everything I had was — what do they call it? Circumstantial evidence? Or clouds in my coffee? Either way, I didn't have diddly-squat. If I didn't get better at this *Magnum P.I.* stuff, I might not make it out of this alive.

About three in the afternoon, Chloe called to say that two dozen red roses had been delivered to the bookstore.

"Who are they from?" Surely not, I thought to myself. No way in hell they could be from...

"Senator Johnson," Chloe cooed. "Oh, Tildy. Do you want me to read the note?"

I did.

"'Roses are red. Violets are blue. If you cover for me, I'll cover for you'." She paused, then, "Tildy, what does that mean?"

"Nothing." I knew I'd answered too quickly. Chloe might be young, but she wasn't stupid. She'd jump all over this if I didn't nip it in the bud. "He's just making a joke about both our bad experiences with the press. That's all. Nothing more. Don't make a big deal out of it."

"Okay," she said slowly, then, "Did you do it with him?"

"Go back to work, Chloe." Oh, swell. Another fine mess.

The more I thought about it, the madder I got. Cover for me? Would that be before or after he called Attanasio and had him sic his goon on me? Would that be before or after he found out that Donnie the Gorilla couldn't finish me off? Cover for me? Right.

I'll show you *cover*, asshole.

"You're going down, Kimosabe. You and..."

Chapter Eighteen

"...the horse you rode in on?"

Big John Yazzie, Sheriff John's father answered, "Frijoles? He's a pinto."

I admired the gorgeous red-and-white pony tied to the corral. "What a beauty."

We sat three or four rows up in the rickety wooden bleachers along one side of the rodeo arena at Chinle, five hundred miles from the middle of nowhere. It was pretty amazing how many people had made the long dusty trek to see the Professional Indian Rodeo Cowboys Association perform their summer Navajo event.

I guess it was a bigger deal than I ever knew, but then I'm a city girl.

The announcer's voice blared out over the loud speaker, "Our first contestants in the chicken pull competition are...."

His voice droned on as two cowboys walked out into the middle of the dusty arena, one carrying a shovel and the other carrying a crazed squawking chicken.

Haggis freaked out, straining against his leash, dying for a shot at that chicken.

"Back, T-Rex, back." I snapped the leash and he settled down to a soft whine, watching intently as the men buried the chicken up to its neck in the loose dirt.

"Aaah, John?" The situation called for tact, but as usual... "What in the sam hill are they doing to that chicken?"

He laughed. "Chicken pull."

"What?"

"It's a contest of horsemanship. The bird gets buried up to the neck and the cowboys gallop past and try to grab it. Whoever gets it, wins."

"Oh, kind of a low-tech Donkey Kong."

"Donkey what?"

A half dozen riders suddenly burst out of the gate and circled the arena at a dead run. The first cowboy broke away and headed straight for the poor bird, slipped sideways in his saddle and grabbed for the chicken's head as he rode past. He missed.

I cheered. Everyone glared at me. Guess I was the sole supporter for the pitiful chicken.

You're probably wondering what I was doing in the middle of the Navajo Nation at a chicken pull. I'm not sure I can explain it, but I'll try. For the last few days it was like I'd been caught in the middle of a whirlwind, everything swirling around, tossing me first this way, then that way, all coming at me at once.

It was information overload but nothing connected. The little voice in my head said that Yazzie's father might be the missing link. So, I called him up and asked if I could see him. He wanted to meet at the rodeo arena which I thought was a pretty cool idea. I'd never been to a rodeo and I might have gone even if I wasn't going to interview him.

I got up at the crack of dawn to do my urban cowgirl schtick with hat, jeans, boots and even a bolo tie. I packed on the make-up to cover my scrapes and bruises. It got to the point where I had to rub some of it off since I was beginning to look like a Kabuki player. But when your face is as banged up as mine was, no matter what they say on TV, Cover Girl doesn't.

It was a helluva long drive out there, almost half of which was "shake and bake," an expression I picked up at the gas station on the road to Chinle. The real-live, walking, talking attendant who actually filled my tank, checked my oil and cleaned the inch and a half of dust off my windshield (service is alive and well and living on the reservation) laughed when I complained about how bad the roads were. He said it was shake-and-bake, that the roads were so bad, first you're shaken to pieces, then baked to a crisp under the blazing desert sun. His advice had been to "just pick a rut and stay in it till you get where you're going." I did, and while it didn't actually make the going any easier, it at least gave me something to do along the way.

A few miles away from the rodeo arena, I got behind this truck full of Navajos. There were four adults in the cab and eight kids in the bed. The kids kept waving and laughing and making funny faces. Haggis hated them and barked indignantly until they literally disappeared in the thick cloud of dust the truck kicked up. I could barely make out the occasional brake light. My windshield wipers scraped the grit around some, but couldn't begin to keep up with it. It was getting hard to breathe, so I switched the A/C over to recirculate, but the dust came in anyway. It had soaked into my pores by then. I'd never be clean again.

Good thing I started out early. By the time I parked in the dirt lot at the rodeo, the three-hour drive had taken four and a half hours. I would never find the car again, since my formerly blue Toyota 4Runner looked just like all the other cars and trucks — covered in heavy layers of red Arizona dirt.

After I rang Mr. Yazzie's cell phone, he and Frijoles met me at the ticket booth.

John Senior was eighty if he was a day. While Sheriff John was a huge man, his father was on the small side. How ironic that Big John was a runt compared to Little John. Gleaming white hair was pulled back in a bun and bound with yarn. He wore a dark blue velvet pullover, Levis and Navajo boots. His necklace was alternating nuggets of drilled turquoise and red coral with a big silver-and-turquoise devil's claw. Massive ornate silver bracelets cuffed each arm. A colorful woven sash patterned with traditional fetishes was wrapped around his waist.

He was a man of influence and standing, a tribal elder and shaman whose wisdom was etched in every crease of his face. His dark eyes were piercing, all-seeing, but not unkind. No way could I lie to those eyes.

So, I shelved my usual elaborate concoction of fibs and came right out with it. "Mr. Yazzie, you don't know me from Geronimo."

He smiled and cocked one wooly white brow. "Good enough for you to make Indian jokes."

"Touché. Here goes. I need to know if your son is now or ever was connected to Ted Cochran or Wade Johnson or the Canyon State Land and Cattle Company."

"No. But I was."

"Get outta here," then, "You?"

"Me." He stood up and held out his hand. "Come with me if you want to hear my story. It is only for your two ears, not these many."

Should I go? Was I stumbling blindly into another trap? But then I looked in his eyes and saw that he'd never hurt me. I was being a wuss, as usual.

I took his surprisingly strong hand and slid across the bench, stifling a scream as a splinter of wood drove itself into my derriere. Mother of pearl, talk about your pain in the butt!

As we walked out of the arena, one of us trying to yank out the phone pole lodged in her left butt cheek, the chicken gave a horrendous squawk. I didn't look back. I didn't want to know. Haggis, on the other hand, was taking in every detail. I'd ask him about it later.

Mr. Yazzie lead me to a big shaded lean-to where picnic tables were set up. Nearby were several food concessions and displays where young women in tee-shirts and jeans and old women in heavy tiered skirts and cotton blouses sold their wares.

Big John brought over a couple of ice-cold colas and a plateful of food. He identified each item on the plate. "Navajo taco. Indian fry bread. Chicken-on-a-stick."

A cheer went up from the crowd at the arena and I decided to pass on the chicken. But the fried bread was real tasty.

Big John fed the chicken to Haggis. The little traitor wolfed it right down.

"Thank you, "I dabbed at the corners of my mouth with a paper napkin. "That was excellent. Did you say it was fried bread?"

"Fry bread," then he added nonchalantly. "My son is not a killer."

Oooh, he was good.

But so was I. "I believe Sheriff John was involved in a murder about twenty-five years ago and I'm not about to just let it go."

"Persistent women aren't easily ignored."

The shaman was putting me on. "Confucius?"

"No. Bill Clinton."

I laughed out loud. What a neat old guy.

Without any warning, he pulled the old two-step shuffle on me. "I dreamed you would come many moons ago."

Many moons ago? Oh, come on.

"Sorry," he said when he saw the look on my face. "I do it for the tourists. Sometimes it gets out of hand. While it's cliché, it's also the truth. I dreamed you'd come, a clumsy redhead asking questions about things long past."

Clumsy? What the heck was he talking about? I'm a friggin' swan — not. But I was really impressed with his intuition.

"My dream forgot to mention you were coming after my son. The answers you seek lie elsewhere. Let me put your feet on the right path. Turn on your recorder."

I did. I didn't want to miss a word.

John's tale came easily like it had been rehearsed many times.

"My son is only a good man with a secret, nothing more. Not a killer. Not a conspirator. A secret can become a lie when it hides something for so long, and maybe he is guilty of that. But John never murdered anyone."

Well, phooey, another theory shot all to hell. "How can you be so sure?"

"There are things I know and things I don't know. This is a thing I know." His resonant voice reminded me of Charleton Heston as Moses — *let my people go!* It added to his ambiance, you didn't want to question anything he said, but...

"So do I. And one of the things I know is that your son and my friend had a secret. And that their secret was a threat to your son."

"Your visions are still incomplete, Matilda." He sighed tiredly. "My son came to me when Houston disappeared."

I stared at him. I'd never said who my friend was.

"John's grief is unending. Houston was the love of his life, and to this day, he still searches for him."

I looked back to that first day in the bookstore when Yazzie came in. I tried to remember his eyes. His voice. I tried to put aside the flash of anger in my vision and see beyond it. What I saw, what I felt, what I remembered was a man in pain. Once again my psychic vision wasn't twenty-twenty. But... "If Sheriff John didn't kill Houston, who did?"

"The spirit of my grandmother told me only of his death, not who was responsible for it."

I was surprised. "You knew Houston was murdered and you never said anything to your own son?"

He shrugged. "If the spirits wanted John to know, they'd have told him, not me."

Hmm. Must be the Indian way.

"And what was your part in all this?"

Sadness emptied his eyes. "Many years ago, I betrayed the land. I betrayed the people. I betrayed myself. Wade Johnson, a man I believed was my friend, had a plan for the Bureau of Land Management to buy thousands of acres of tribal land dirt cheap and re-sell it to his friends in Phoenix. He promised if I convinced the tribe to sell, the rewards would be jobs, a hospital, a school," he paused and, for the first time, looked away, "and my son would become Sheriff."

He drained his cola, and stared down into the cup, his brow creased, his eyes troubled.

I found myself holding my breath. He was about to break this whole thing wide open and it was all I could do not to grab him and shake the truth out of him.

A half-dozen women wearing elaborate costumes covered in metal cones walked by. The small cones rubbed together as they moved, jingling like sleigh bells. It was a happy sound, like Christmas, at odds with the dark subject.

He rubbed his hand over his face and continued, "We sold it cheap. Might as well have given us glass beads. Wade got what he wanted — money and power. Ted Cochran got what he wanted — money and land. There was no hospital. No school. They bought my son's badge to guarantee my silence.

"I've kept my tongue all these years to protect John and to preserve the pride he brings my people. So much has been taken from us; he's our shining hope. It's all we got out of this.

"They managed to hide it all these years. But the time's come for these things to be made known. The ownership is buried in deeds under many different names." He removed a tattered piece of paper from his pocket and handed it to me. "Search the records for land titled under these names."

Wow. What a story. Houston would love it. "Why tell me?"

"Because I'm a selfish old man who's tired of hiding the past. You'll be the one to find the truth and deliver justice..."

...and the American way, I thought to myself. It's a bird, it's a plane....

"Nobody likes a smartass, Matilda. This is serious."

I gawked at him.

He pointed his finger in my face. "Now go back home and get to work."

"Y-y-yes, sir," I stammered and clicked off the tape recorder as he walked away.

"Oh," he turned. "One more thing."

I looked up and saw him standing in the sun, casting a long shadow for such a small man. Was that his aura? Or was it just the angle of the sun bathing him in that golden glow?

"Cochran has another secret. There's something buried on his land. Check out the ninth-hole putting green."

"Something? What? A body?" Oh my God. Could it be Houston? "Who is it?" I called to his back.

He kept walking, laughing softly. "If the spirits wanted you to know, they would have told you, not me."

Maybe he oughta take that routine on the road.

I felt pretty good at the way things had gone. I bought every word Mr. Yazzie had said — that Sheriff John wasn't a murderer, that Wade Johnson and Ted Cochran were in fact responsible for the land scam which caused Bolles' murder and probably Houston's — and also that there was something buried on Cochran's golf course that would bring all this to a head.

I had solved the case — I just knew it.

But there was nothing quite like evidence you could see and touch and dig up. On my way back to Sedona, I decided to make a stop at the County Recorder's office in Flagstaff to check out the land deeds John had said would tie the principals to the scam.

But first, I had another mission. It involved the crate of chickens behind the corrals.

I took Haggis to the car, fastened him in his seat belt and opened the moon roof so he'd have plenty of air. He was pissed, but that's life. I'd just have to make it up to him later.

I snuck up on the crate stealthily, humming the *Mission Impossible* theme. I was quick. I was light. I was the wind. It's hard to be the wind when the oppressed victims make a racket that would wake the dead.

The latch on the crate was nothing more than a loop of wire over a nail head. Piece of cake (heard that one before?). The door swung open and the chickens moseyed on out, blinking their eyes, clucking their relief. It would have been a clean break if not for that pesky sheepdog who came bounding over, gleefully rounded them up, then herded the little suckers back as fast as I could shoo them away, even managing to close the cage back up.

The sheepdog (or should I say chicken dog?) sat there with a smug look on his face, panting and grinning and patting himself on the darn back for a job well done.

"Smarty pants," I muttered, then to the birds. "Stupid chickens. You shoulda run when you had the chance."

On my way back to the car, I passed the Chicken-On-A-Stick booth. This time I stopped and brought one and fed it to Haggis.

* * * * *

Canyon de Chelly is God's summer residence, and even more wondrously unexpected if you don't know you're going there. The golden afternoon sun casts an unearthly glow over the mahogany-varnished sandstone cliffs which rise to meet a blue blue sky. Piñon pines and juniper trees dot the upper rim. In the canyon below cottonwoods cluster along a slow-flowing creek.

I'd taken the South Rim Drive for a little sightseeing before making my way back to civilization. Then, guess what? Wrong-Turn Tildy strikes again. One look at canyon walls above, not below me, and I knew I wasn't in Kansas any more, or even on the South Rim Drive. Somehow I'd managed to wind up at the bottom of Canyon de Chelly.

I spread the map and tried to figure out where we were while Haggis stared grumpily out the window, still ticked about being left in the car and missing all the fun with the chickens. Plus, I figured he might be having déjà vu out here in the toolies and worries over being abandoned again.

"Don't worry, Haggis. I won't leave you. Not out here. Not anywhere. Not ever. You and me, we're joined at the hip, pal."

He smiled and wagged his tail and barked as if to say: Okay, now that's settled, let's go home.

And I would have loved to. Really. If only... "I don't suppose you know the way?"

He looked like he might be reconsidering what John Yazzie said about me being a clumsy redhead.

"Guess not," I said. "Me either."

As the wise man once said, "If the spirits wanted you to know where you were going..."

Chapter Nineteen

"...they should have told you." The young Navajo Tour Leader crossed his arms and stepped away from my car. "You can't come down here, lady, not without an Indian guide. There's quicksand, flash floods, cougars, bears. Lady, you get stuck out here and no one would find you for a long time."

I totally agreed with him. "Not to mention those guys." I peered through the dirty windshield at the turkey buzzards perched in a tree, salivating. "Look, mister. I want to get out of here as much you want me out. Just point me in the right direction and I'm history."

"No, I'll have to lead you out." His badge said he was an Official Navajo Tour Guide for Dineh Canyon Tours. Who did he think he was kidding? He didn't look old enough to drive, let alone be official.

But official or not, he certainly had a good opinion of himself. He puffed up his chest and gestured pompously at the six-wheel open-bed truck parked smack behind me. "What am I supposed to tell them? Probably lose at least an hour out of my schedule."

I craned my neck for a look. The dozen cranky tourists in the rear (of what looked more like a troop carrier than a tour bus) were taking on the threatening demeanor of a Gestapo hit squad.

"I don't know." I thought a minute, then fished in my purse and came up with a fifty-dollar bill. "Tell them the drinks are on the house?"

* * * * *

We drove slowly along the washboard dirt trail, the Nazis in front, Haggis and I behind.

An enormous stone monolith came into view and the truck stopped. I pulled up behind it and got out to see what the problem was. Only it wasn't a problem, it was one of the local tourist attractions.

The young Navajo glared at me as he explained to his group, "Spider Rock is eight hundred feet high. It's the home of the legendary Spider Woman, who's said to live at the very top, waiting and hoping for Navajo children to misbehave, then she spins a web and swoops down to eat them. The white coating around the top of the spire is the bleached bones of all the naughty children she's eaten...." He looked me right in the eye and smiled as he said, "Alive."

I saw how it was with him and got back in the car, even if I thought he was being unreasonable. Hell, I gave him fifty bucks. A little folklore and local color wasn't asking too much.

I noticed a cloud of dust and a dark vehicle in my rearview mirror. It seemed to be coming pretty fast. Suddenly the place was like rush hour on the Hollywood Freeway.

I turned to Haggis. "So, you think *he's* got an Indian guide?" Yeah, I was kinda bitchy. But I figured I was entitled.

By the time, *my* Indian guide had lead me back to the South Rim Drive, the other vehicle had caught up and was tailing fairly close. It was a black four-wheel-drive Ford Excursion, you know, the ones that look like an office building on wheels.

When the Navajo guide waved me back onto the main road, the Excursion followed while the tourists turned around and headed back down into the canyon.

I picked up a little speed on the paved road and was tooling along, just minding my own business, concentrating on not getting lost again — God knows I didn't want to alienate the official Indian guides any more than I already had — when BAM! The friggin' Excursion slammed into my rear bumper.

"What in...?" I fought the urge to oversteer and managed to keep the car on the road.

Now I'm willing to give anybody the benefit of the doubt. But — no doubt about it, this was no accident. The guy was trying to kill me. How did I know? Because he came at me again, rammed me from the side this time, sending me spinning.

I hung on for dear life as the car careened crazily around and around in the loose gravel, closer and closer to the edge of the cliff. Oh Jesus! Two wheels off now and still skittering along the million-foot dropoff.

Poor little Haggis was scared and whimpering.

Poor little Tildy was scared and screaming bloody murder.

Suddenly, I was back on the road. "Thank you God. I'll give up chocolate for Lent."

WHAM! It slammed up against me again — like being hit by a train. If it hadn't been for Haggis' seatbelt, the jolt would have launched him.

I squinted to see who was trying to kill me, but no luck. The windows were tinted so dark they were nearly opaque. It was spooky, a ghost car without a driver. A Ford on a mission from hell.

But it wasn't a ghost at all. It had to be our local zoo escapee — the three-hundred-pound gorilla.

He kept pushing. I kept pushing back, but he was bigger and he was heavier and I was definitely losing the battle. We raced along, door to door, rubbing against each other.

I could feel my car going sideways. No matter which way I steered, no matter how hard I braked, no matter how much I accelerated or down shifted, nothing did any good. I was totally at his mercy. He pushed; and I went sailing — right over the edge.

For what seemed like an eternity we were airborne and all I could see was blue blue sky.

I locked my elbows, gripped the wheel, and screamed, "Hang on, Haggis!"

A bunch of thick green bushes rose up to meet my windshield and we plowed into them. I grunted. Haggis yelped and the car shuddered in protest. Branches scraped along the doors, screeching like fingernails on a chalkboard.

There wasn't even time to draw a breath before we plummeted down. This time the car hit with a spine-shattering jolt. I heard the sound of snapping metal — Ouch! That can't be good.

And then we were rolling and careening out of control over the rugged terrain.

My inner voice cried: Steer, you fool. You can do it!

I cried back, "No I can't! Do it yourself."

But I held on somehow, navigating like a Formula One driver as we bucked, bounced and slid all the way down, rocks pounding the undercarriage like cannonballs. Suddenly, we were at the bottom: wheels down, tits up. But it wasn't over yet.

I tried to stop but — NO BRAKES! We plunged into a stand of saplings, mowing them down, and came blindly barreling out the other side straight into a small herd of grazing sheep.

Haggis barked in alarm.

It was like an obstacle course. Hard left. Sharp right. Oh, Lord, there's another one. I cranked the wheel and managed to avoid every single sheep, some just by inches.

Haggis barked again.

"Calm down. I didn't hit them. They're alive!" Which might be more than I could say for us if I didn't get the car stopped.

I saw the creek in front of us and had a brainstorm.

The water might slow us down. We splashed into the muddy water and bounded up the other side, and we did slow down — a lot. But my poor car was wheezing and rattling worse than old Joe ever did. Then, we cleared the slope and landed hard —

Holy Mother of God!.

Did I say brainstorm? Make that a *brainfart*. We came down nose to nose with the friggin' Excursion.

"Persistent sonvabitch."

I spun the wheel and held it all the way to the left. The rear end fishtailed, then the tires dug in and we threw a blanket of red dust all over the black Excursion.

I took off.

He took off right behind me.

We blasted over every damn rut, across every damn wash and through every damn bush in the valley; and still the guy came. Shit. I felt like Butch Cassidy, or maybe the Sundance Kid (I always liked him better). What was it going to take to get this jerk off my ass?

I was heading back toward the creek and had barely started across, when as plain as day, I heard a shout: "Veer right. NOW!"

Without even thinking about it, I jerked the wheel. The back end slid out, sending me in a wide curving arc across the creek. We bogged down and finally stopped in water up to the wheel wells. The engine coughed once and died. I cranked it, again and again, but it was no good.

The Excursion came barreling across like death on wheels, spraying jets of water at least ten feet out the sides.

My car still wouldn't start and now it was too late. I put my head in my hands. I couldn't bear to look. "Omigod, we screwed the pooch."

Haggis yipped indignantly.

I didn't think he was grasping the seriousness of the situation.

That's when I heard it. A dull thud and the sound of tires whipping mud into a frothy mess. I looked up in time to see the black devil sinking in quicksand all the way to the windows. The same quicksand I'd have hit if not for my nagging inner voice.

"Well, good."

Not in a charitable mood, I tried my car, and when it turned over, I breathed a sigh of relief and drove out of the creek and down the rutted track. As I rounded the corner, I turned to Haggis and said, "Sorry about the pooch remark."

The sound of an approaching vehicle echoed through the canyon and I held my breath in dread. But it was only my Official Indian Guide and his troop of Nazis. I stopped the car and jumped out to greet them.

He wasn't nearly as glad to see me as I was him. I could tell by the way he stomped over, took a good look at my car and asked, "This ought to be good. What's your story this time?"

Well, I gotta tell you that really let the air out of my sails. I'd been through a lot that day. And this guy has the nerve to ask what's my story?

When I was in high school I won a ribbon for poetry. Now, granted the competition wasn't what you call stiff, it was just me and Stanley, the class nerd with buck teeth and thick glasses. But, just so you know, I *am* a poet. And as indignant as I was at that very moment, I guess it kicked in, because...

"You want a story? I got your story right here."

His jaw dropped as I recited:

"The ghost first gave me a pretty good fright.
Then the Bee Gees kept me up all night.
There's your Elvis freak,
your Congressional geek.
And I barely escaped
from the Mafia ape.
The chickens and ants were a pain in the neck.
And now...

Chapter Twenty

...me and my car and my life are a wreck."

Sob.

I hadn't meant to cry. Really. I didn't cry when I told my story to the Navajo Guide. But there was just something empathetic about Sheriff John that made those tears of self-pity well up.

We were parked on the shoulder of Highway 160 still about seventy-five miles outside of Flagstaff. That was as far as I'd been able to inch-worm along in the rain and the dark with no lights and sporadic brakes.

Yazzie had pulled me over and walked up to the car, ticket book in hand.

What the heck was he going to cite me for? Certainly not for speeding! I rolled my window down and heard him muttering, "What kind of idiot would take this piece of shit out on the road?" He shone his flashlight in my face. "Oh my God, Miss MacNamara. Are you all right? Is this from last night? Or were you re-injured just now?"

Oh, yeah, my Technicolor face. "It's from last night, Sheriff."

A car whizzed by, drenching him in dirty water. He was in an ugly mood. "And what the hell happened to the car? You get in a debate with a semi or a freight train? Didn't anyone tell you they always win? What a mess."

That did it. The tears and the poetry flowed.

His expression had softened by the time I'd finished. I thought maybe he was a little teary-eyed himself (but I couldn't really tell in the rain). "That was lovely," he said.

And I cried harder.

He reached in and patted my shoulder. "It's okay, Miss MacNamara. I'm not gonna write you up."

Like I even cared at that point.

"But," he shook his head, "I gotta call a tow truck to haul you in. No way you can drive this car on a public highway. It's a hazard. No brakes. Frame's bent. Lights out. I can't even begin to list all the things wrong with it. It's a total loss."

I sniffed and ran my hand over the dash. "A total loss?" Not my poor little 4Runner. "But the new-car smell hasn't even worn off yet."

I waited with Haggis in Sheriff John's warm, dry patrol car. Haggis curled up in my lap and went to sleep. How the heck could he snooze at a time like that?

Sheriff John didn't say much while he wrote up his report. Every so often he'd ask me a question about the "incident." As outrageous as the whole thing was, he never even blinked — just nodded and kept writing.

He got on the radio and called the Navajo police. They radioed back that the Dineh tour guide had reported my little problem and they'd gone to check it out. By the time they got there the Excursion was up to its roof in quicksand and it would have to stay there until morning.

They wouldn't find anything. I was sure of it. Donnie was long gone, and probably back on my trail already.

He was quickly becoming my Michael Meyers.

* * * * *

It turned out that Little John was my knight in shining armor. It was easy to see why Houston fell in love with him.

Not only did he find a doggie-friendly Best Western, he helped me check in, settle Haggis in his crate, then walked me next door to Denny's. All I'd had to eat was the fry bread, which was a long time and a lot of used calories ago.

Over scrambled eggs, hash browns, biscuits and gravy, John Yazzie and I became friends and enemies at the same time.

We talked easily about replacing my car (Yazzie figured it was too far gone to fix). We talked about my bad marriage. We talked about his job. And then he finally got around to what was really on his mind.

"Why would you drive all the way to Chinle to see my father?"

Should I tell him? Which part? How much? Would he even believe me? It was a dicey situation. On the one hand you have Sheriff John Yazzie, who would be interested in the criminal aspects. On the other hand, you have John Yazzie the man, who would be interested in the personal aspects.

I chose the man. "Houston sends his love."

He choked on his coffee and it was a minute before he could talk. "Did you say...?"

I nodded, "Houston sends his love."

"Where is he? Can I see him? Why hasn't he called or written or..." The poor man was beside himself.

"It's hard to explain."

His mouth tightened. "Well, try, Tildy. Try real hard."

The story came out slowly at first, then faster and faster and I realized I'd been dying to tell someone, anyone, and who better than someone else who loved Houston?

He listened closely, an expression of polite interest glued on his face. Every once in a while there would be this barely perceptible twitch in his right eye, and occasionally he'd looked around at the other tables to see if anyone else was paying attention.

When I'd told it all, soup to nuts, he cleared his throat and said, "Well."

I can tell you exactly where I lost him. It was at the very beginning. The man probably thought I was Looney Tunes — thought, hell, he was pretty damn sure by now. I'd be lucky if he didn't drive me straight to the nearest funny farm.

I felt the need to win him to our side. It was what Houston would want. "I know it's hard to believe, John. But it's true, every word. Ask your dad. He knows."

It was only a minute before the look of stunned disbelief changed to one of complete understanding. I sighed in relief, certain I'd won him over, until he said, "My father. You're like my father. I should have put it together earlier. Psychic book stores. Ghosts. It's the same as his medicine-man hocus-pocus."

"No, John. Please listen to me."

I was losing him, literally. He stood up and dropped some bills on the table. "It's time I got back on the road, Miss MacNamara. And God knows, you need your rest."

"I promised Houston I'd find his murderer. John, listen. He can't cross over until I do. He's in limbo. He's suffering."

Maybe I'd gone too far. The look on his face was raw pain. His eyes were haunted. "Houston's just missing, Miss MacNamara. He's not dead."

He turned on his heel and stalked out.

I walked back to the motel in the rain.

I let Haggis out of his crate and fed him the leftover biscuits and gravy I'd brought him from Denny's. I was still doing penance for the day's disasters.

My cell phone rang. I answered it hesitantly, not knowing who to expect on the other end. "Hello?" I croaked.

"Matilda? It's Andrew." Shock shut me up, so he went on. "Is this a bad time?"

Well, it ain't good. "I was almost killed in the car today." Don't ask me where that came from. The words just leaped out all by themselves. I was doing it again, exposing my soft underbelly.

But just as I was about to make a complete fool of myself, he did the honorable thing and showed his true colors. "Why is it always about you, Matilda? Huh? I call you to tell you I broke up with Elizabeth. My life is falling apart here. I'm suffering, dammit. And all you can do is whine about some little fender bender."

Pucker up, butthole. "I have to go now."

"What?"

I took the rest of my fear and insecurity and sucked it up like the bitter medicine it was. I'd deal with it later. Right then I had to get off the phone. The bastard was making things worse.

Say good night, Gracie.

"Good night, Gracie." And I hung up.

I stripped down to take a shower. A nice hot Jacuzzi was what I really could have used, but I'd have to settle for a hot shower. As I walked past the closet door, I caught a glimpse in the full-length mirror and shrieked at what I saw.

My body was a poor bruised, scabby mess. Besides the swell black eye and blue-and-green fingermarks on my neck, there was a big old red welt across my chest from the seat belt. The palms of my hands and both knees were scabby from falling down in Wade Johnson's driveway. When I turned around to check out the ant welts on my butt, I moaned at the festering wound in my butt cheek where the telephone pole had been lodged. One good thing, I'd have some terrific battle scars to show off to my grandchildren — if I ever had any.

Haggis sat beside me, his head cocked to one side, checking out my lumps and bumps.

"Pretty gruesome, huh, pal?"

He nodded in agreement.

I turned on the shower and let it heat up a few minutes, while I tried to figure an angle on how to convince Sheriff John to help me. So far, my best sales efforts sucked.

I reached down and scratched Haggis under his chin. It was his favorite spot.

"You know what, sweetie. It's a damn good thing Mommy's asshole ex-husband made a lot of money, because Mommy couldn't even sell ice water in hell. Not even if..."

Chapter Twenty-One

"...the water fountain is broken and so is the cola machine in the lobby." Shirley Smith, according to her name plate, was a heavyset lady with a head full of over-processed apricot hair, and one of the most awful red-and-yellow tent dresses in the history of mankind. She shoved aside a stack of papers on the counter, making room for her ample bosoms and a box full of microfiche records. "You'll have to wade through this bunch to get to land deeds as far back as you wanna go, deary." She pointed to the readers across the room. "Have a nice day."

People always say that, but what they really mean is: Now leave me the hell alone. "Thanks, deary," I called sweetly and plopped my butt down.

The Coconino County Clerk's office was a hell hole. No A/C. No breeze stirred through the open windows. It was only ten a.m. but already pushing ninety with the humidity at about four hundred per cent. The fold-up chair was brutal against my inflamed butt. And with nothing to drink, I'd for sure have to forego the Three Musketeers bar in my purse. It was shaping up to be a long day.

But in the end, it was a complete success.

Big John's list named several companies that held deeds on enormous plots in the area just south and west of Sedona. They'd been smart. And they'd been thorough. But if you peeled back enough layers, you'd eventually find them. And I did. Ponderosa Pines Realty was a holding company for EBS Land Development which was principally owned by Kirkland Enterprises. Kirkland Enterprises was partially held by Candyland Entertainment whose president was none other than Ellen Johnson, the Senator's buxom ex-wife. The same magic act concealed none other than Ted Cochran behind the facade of Manchester Trading Company.

The holder of the largest section of land had me stumped for a while. La Bella Vineyards in Sonoma County was owned by two men whose names sounded as vaguely familiar to me as they probably do to you. John Smith and Tom Brown. Hmm. Aliases, ya think? But who were they really? It wasn't hard to figure out when I noticed the last page listed their mailing address in Phoenix. It was an address I knew. One I'd been to. One I wouldn't forget as long as I freakin' lived. It was Joe Attanasio's house.

I finally managed to connect the dots and the end result was a picture of three big bad wolves — Cochran, Johnson and Attanasio in bed together with the covers pulled up to their chinny-chin-chins.

Gotcha, dudes.

I printed it out, all of it, every cross-reference, every last word, paid the fees to Shirley, who was sweating profusely (and unattractively) by then, gave her back her box of microfiche, and went my merry way.

I was so pleased with the way things went, that I walked over to the Jack in the Box across the street, bought a piece of chocolate cake and Super Quencher diet cola. I took the drink back to poor old frizzed-out Shirley at the Recorder's office.

"Here you go, deary."

She was caught completely off guard.

"Have a nice day," I said and walked down to wait for my ride.

The first thing that morning, the insurance adjuster had called and taken a statement over the phone. I did most of the talking. There seemed to be a lot of long silences at the other end. Before hanging up, I made a twelve-thirty appointment to go with him to see my car.

It wasn't quite time for him to pick me up, so I waited in the shade and wolfed down my chocolate cake which was starting to melt in the heat. In the wink of an eye, there was gooey chocolate everywhere. A big trout fountain spewed water from its mouth on the steps of the county building. Ignoring the "no bathing" sign and the steely-eyed stare of the landscaper, I held my hands under the spray. It was the first time I'd ever washed in fish spit.

Just then, a brown Chevy S10 Blazer pulled up. Must be my ride. I dried my hands on my jeans and hurried over.

The passenger window slid down. "Ms. MacNamara?" The man was in his thirties, with short brown hair, wearing aviator sunglasses and a blue Oxford shirt.

"Are you Mister...?"

"Flake. James Flake." The Bond theme played in my head as he handed me his card. "Claims adjuster."

I glanced at the card as I opened the door. "Thanks for picking me up."

"Not a problem. Part of the job. Hop in." His sentences were rapid fire.

Before I even had my seatbelt fastened, he was pulling away from the curb, driving like a man late for an appointment — slamming on his brakes at every red light, flooring it at every green light.

I dug my fingers into the armrest, wondering if I'd have to file a bodily injury claim against my own claims guy.

James the Flake executed a hairpin turn at full speed, then tore across the parking lot of my old stomping grounds, the local Sam's Club, where he ricocheted off every speed bump in the place at forty miles an hour.

While my teeth knocked together at every jolt, I managed to grit out, "The Lord is my shepherd..."

"You a religious woman, Miss MacNamara?"

"I am now," I squeaked. "Look out!"

I ducked my head as James jerked the wheel to miss side-swiping a guy with a big flatbed cart loaded with at least twenty cases of pop. The guy jumped out of the way. The cart slammed into the solid concrete base of a street lamp. The impact sent the cases of soda flying.

Pop geysered like old Faithful. It was a sight to behold.

"...yea, though I walk through the Valley of the Shadow of Death..."

After hopscotching over the railroad tracks, we roared through the tow lot gates. James stood on the brakes and we jerked to a stop in front of the office.

I leaped out and crossed myself. "Amen."

A shirtless middle-aged grease monkey, covered with a zillion tattoos (too bad I didn't have time to do the art tour just then), ambled out and lead us over to my Toyota 4Runner. Or what was left of it. In the daylight I could see how bad the damage was. Big scrape marks along the side, front end smashed in, front wheels sprung, bumper hanging off, and tree limbs jammed in the undercarriage. Not to mention the damage I couldn't see. It made me really sad. It was the first car I'd really bought on my own. It was the first car I'd really thought of as mine.

"Oh, poor baby, just look at you." I ran my hand over the dented door.

The grease monkey hawked up a wad then spat. "Yep. Fubar."

"Foo what?" I asked.

"Fucked up beyond all recognition," he recited. "Fubar."

I stared at my little car in dismay, checked out the hundreds of other demolished vehicles, then turned back to the grease monkey. "I can see you're a connoisseur, sir, and an expert judge of such matters."

James set his laptop on the hood, opened it up, and said pompously, "I'll be the judge of that."

He walked around the car inspecting the damage, then logging it into his laptop.

"Don't do that!" he yelled as a piece of chrome molding I barely touched clattered to the ground.

"Sorry." I shoved it under the car with my foot.

"When you gave me your statement, you said you were run off the road by a Mafia gorilla."

"Yes. The same mafioso that did this to me two nights ago." I pointed to my face.

"If that's true " — What did he mean: if that's true? — "why did you wait three hours to officially report the incident?"

"I told the Official Indian Guide. Doesn't that make it official?"

"No — you make an official report to a law enforcement officer. You know what a law enforcement officer is? A cop. A highway patrolman. A sheriff's deputy."

Maybe I was a little grumpy from sleeping in a strange bed, and getting run off the road and crashing into a bottomless pit and nearly dying, but I didn't like his attitude, not one little bit. "Thanks for sharing, Mr. Flake," then, "What's bothering you? Just say it."

"I'm wondering if there ever was a gorilla. I'm wondering if maybe it wasn't a cow, instead?" He asked shrewdly, "Did you hit a cow, Miss MacNamara?"

"You don't believe me!" I was dumbstruck, well, not quite. "That sucks! It's...it's..." I looked at the grease monkey.

"Fubar," he smiled, displaying a mouth full of hillbilly teeth.

"Yeah. That." The bastard had gone and hurt my feelings. "You ask Sheriff John Yazzie. Ask the Navajo Police. Ask Chief Bill Parrish of the Sedona Police Department. They'll tell you." What a jackass. "I'm outta here." I asked the grease monkey, "Can I use your phone to call a taxi?"

"Why it would be my pleasure, ma'am."

I turned on my heel and stalked off.

"You go, girl," the grease monkey called.

James added his two cents, "I'm going to catagorize you as a high risk and recommend your insurance company raise your rates."

Without even turning around, I called back, "Only assholes are petty."

"And only morons walk around with chocolate smeared all over their face."

Damn. The smug bastard one-upped me.

* * * * *

That afternoon I bought a brand new Atlantis-blue Toyota Land Cruiser with oak leather interior and all the bells and whistles including, boys and girls, a DVD-based navigation system with a seven-inch display.

According to the salesman, the navigation system with GPS locator, the fulltime four-wheel-drive system with locking center differential, active track TRAC 4-wheel traction control and vehicle skid-control system would not only keep me from ever getting lost again, I could go anywhere my little heart desired. I could go on the shake and bake. I could trek down to Canyon De Chelly (only with an official Indian guide of course), even...

Chapter Twenty-Two

...the ninth-hole green of Cochran's Paradise Resort golf course. The night air was alive with the scent of cedars. A marigold moon played hide and seek among the clouds. Strains of *Moon River* drifted from the nearby club house. The grass was moist velvet beneath our feet, and the red earth was...

"A real ball-buster!" Chloe was not a happy camper.

She had done a complete one-eighty from gung ho for high adventure to scared shitless of getting caught. It was pretty amazing considering she was the one who'd convinced Joaquin to join us on our mission impossible.

Joaquin, at first, had worried about getting hauled off to jail but, in the end, chivalry won out over good judgment — chivalry and the not-to-be-missed chance to look sexy and dangerous as a pirate in head-to-toe black. Yes, us womenfolk have to be looked after and no reason a macho dude shouldn't look good doing it.

It was already dark before I got back from Flagstaff, and instead of going home, I drove straight to the book store. Maybe Sheriff John wouldn't help me solve Houston's murder, but I was pretty sure I knew two people who would. So I told Chloe and Joaquin everything, start to finish, blood and guts, the whole enchilada. And, like I said, Chloe was hot for the idea.

"A murder?" she chirped, "Ohmigod. That's so cool."

"I am only interested in live bodies, bella," Joaquin declared.

"But it's for a good cause," I cajoled. "Please." And it was the gospel truth. What better cause than to be able to go home that night and tell Houston I'd found his grave and his murderer, and he could wing his way to Heaven any time he felt like it?

In the end, they both agreed to go, although they made it quite clear it was not for humanitarian reasons. It was because they'd never hear the end of it if they didn't do it, plus I agreed to pay them time-and-a-half. They also made me promise that if we got caught, I'd not only pay them for their stint in jail, but also post bail and even pay for the lawyer. I promised (after all, it's only money) and off we all went.

Chloe supplied two shovels, hand-chosen for her monthly gold-prospecting weekends. I supplied the pickaxe, left over from the "gopher holes" in the apple orchard the last time I was looking for Houston's body. And Joaquin supplied the muscle — enough said. He swung the pick ax easily, and both Chloe and I forgot to dig while the sweat trickled down his flexing, sinewy chest and over his six-pack abs. Did I forget to mention he'd taken off the black shirt after the first half hour, and that he was using the pirate bandana to wipe the sweat from his brow, so Joaquin's loose hair cascaded over his tawny shoulders? Here was a man who belonged on the cover of a steamy romance novel. Here was a man who put even Fabio to shame. Yes, it had been a very long time since I'd been laid.

Chloe's enthusiasm wore off early when her hands blistered from the shovel and her back stiffened up. And then when the moon slid behind a cloud, and we were enveloped in sudden darkness, Chloe freaked out, hypersensitive to every little thing.

At every chirp, every rustle, every animal howl, she'd stop and stare into the darkness. "Shh! Did you hear that? What is it?"

On the other hand, Joaquin had found his rhythm and was really getting into it. "Predators of the night, Chloe."

Swing. Thunk. "A full moon."

Dig in. Pull back. "The witching hour. Vampires. Werewolves."

Chloe stood stock still and began to tremble. "Stop it, Joaquin. Just stop it. You know I believe in that stuff."

His voice was velvet in the night. "Oh, little Chloe, don't be afraid. I'll protect you. That is until they tear out my throat and suck my blood." He swung the garden tool like a battle ax. "Back, demons. Back, I say."

"Ssshhh," I hissed. "Someone's going to hear us."

"That's not funny, Joaquin," Chloe said tightly and threw a clod of dirt at him as he battled imaginary monsters.

I didn't know if I believed in werewolves and vampires like she did, but as dark and eerie as it was out there, better to not tempt fate by offering up your throat. A chill rippled through me as the howl of a faraway coyote pierced the night.

But then the moon came out from behind the cloud and it was just another summer night. Back to work.

"All right, children," I scolded. "Let's just find what we came after and get the hell out of here."

They both went back to digging, but I was beginning to think it would be a miracle if we found anything at all.

The dirt mounds littering the heretofore immaculate ninth green weren't the work of crazed gophers. Chloe, Joaquin and I had been hard at work for hours to get this moon-crater effect. And so far, that's all we'd gotten. All those holes and nothing to show for it, except Ted Cochran's wrath if he ever found out who destroyed his tournament-class golf course.

And that's when — CLUNK — Joaquin's pick hit something solid.

He stopped, threw his hair back over his magnificent shoulders, and smiled up at me, his teeth flashing in the night, "You ask, milady. I find."

I'd have to swoon over this gorgeous hunk later; the matter at hand was more important. Well, maybe not more important, but definitely more at hand.

Chloe and I shone our flashlights down into the hole where Joaquin was bent over, picking up -

What? The answer to Houston's mystery? The key to Attanasio's undoing? A thighbone? Or...

"Just a piece of pottery." Joaquin held it up.

Not exactly the miracle I was hoping for.

Then, Chloe shrieked and jumped back, and for a minute I thought she was fooling around, until she pointed her flashlight at a round object which shone smooth and white at Joaquin's feet.

A blinding flash and the sun is shining in my eyes. The ninth hole is gone, replaced by the virgin desert of yesterday. I'm alone by the creek with a young Indian woman and her papoose. She sings softly to the baby as she kneels to pick blackberries in the shadow of the red rocks.

Here we go again, one of those waking dreams. What does this one mean? Where will it take me?

A spine-chilling snarl shatters the serenity. The woman freezes, then half-turns toward the sound, easing a knife from her belt. She starts to rise. The cougar springs and...

...Chloe screamed, "Oh, my God, it's...

Chapter Twenty-Three

"...against the law." It was the voice of doom, alias Sheriff John. Busted.

Too priceless. Three desperados caught red-handed digging up the most exclusive golf club in Sedona and holding, of all things, a skull.

"I can explain," I offered, then, "Wait a minute — where'd you come from, anyway? Why didn't we hear you sneaking up on us?"

"It's an Indian thing," he said dryly. "And a cop thing. And, boy, are you in trouble."

"But, John," I motioned to Joaquin and he handed me the dirt encrusted skull. "It might be Houston."

He stopped in his tracks and stared at me, his eyes shadowed and hard to read in the moonlight. "Don't be ridiculous." But there was no conviction in his voice.

"It could be." Its energy told me otherwise and I said sadly, "But it isn't."

It was the skull of the Indian woman savaged by the cougar two centuries ago, and that's what I told them.

"Bummer," Chloe was disappointed, but adamant. "You don't understand, Sheriff. We're looking for the body of a murdered reporter. We just have to keep looking. He's here somewhere."

"Not tonight, you won't," Yazzie warned, taking out his cuffs. "Not if you know what's good for you."

That was enough for me. "Okay. Fine. We'll just be on our way then. Uh, what about...?"

I held out the skull.

"Give me that." He was definitely put out.

Joaquin climbed out of the hole and casually shrugged his massive shoulders into his shirt. I don't want to sound bitchy, but I swear Sheriff John was drooling.

Joaquin was laid back, he was cool, he was brilliant when he said, "If that's who milady says, it means centuries ago this place was a sacred burial site. Now I'm not familiar with such things, but it seems to me that perhaps Mr. Cochran built his hotel and his golf course on protected land. Wouldn't the Navajo tribe be interested in knowing that? And wouldn't there be dire consequences to Mr. Cochran if the world learned this?"

John didn't say anything for the longest time, then he smiled, and I saw another brief glimpse of the man Houston loved. "Looks like you three might get to sleep in your own beds tonight, after all."

No way this could be that easy. "Should we...?" I pointed at the holes.

John turned away. "Go on home. Don't worry about them." He added smugly, "I'm gonna love telling old Cochran he might have a zoning problem with his little motel here."

And that was the end of our night raid on the Cochran's Paradise Resort ninth-hole green. We packed up our shovels and left, not even feeling guilty about the dozen or so craters we left out behind. I just hoped some poor little old myopic golf fanatic didn't fall in —

FORE!

The bottom line is: After all the shenanigans he'd pulled, Cochran was overdue for a taste of his own medicine.

I slept like a rock that night with my security system set to blast at even the slightest movement, my Mace clutched in my fist, and my bat under my pillow. I was ready-Freddy if Donnie the Gorilla showed up. But he didn't.

* * * * *

When the morning light slants through the huge cottonwood tree in my back yard, it turns the grass a wonderful emerald green. The birds twitter and coo. Down at the bottom of the hill you can hear the creek gurgling. It's quiet, calming. That time of morning I take my coffee, a chocolate chip muffin and the latest who-dunnit outside and soak it all up.

"I can't believe it was the butler!" I read the last page and closed the book. "He seemed like such a nice guy." My investigative skills definitely weren't what they should be.

But on second thought, a year ago I didn't have any at all. In fact, a year ago my skills in general were pretty limited. Oh sure, I could plan a cocktail party that would knock your socks off. I was a "B" player at a tough tennis club and my serve was legendary. I held my own idling away the time with my rich-and-famous friends, but I fit in with that crowd like a size eight foot in a size six shoe. To be honest, my speciality was letting Andrew the Anus belittle me.

That was then. This is now. And just look at me. I run my own business. It's even profitable. I'm equally adept at interviewing criminals and hobnobbing with the Mafia. I've become somewhat of a weird-ass combo of Mata Hari, Dana Scully and Jessica Fletcher. Who knew?

Two years ago I could barely drive to the mall, much less down the side of a mountain. I was no good at conversing with politicians — forget about seducing them. The only gunfire I ever heard was at the cineplex; and the only mafioso I even knew about was Brando. Go ahead. *Make me an offer I can't refuse.* I can handle it. I can handle it just fine.

I jumped to my feet and belted out, *"I am woman. Hear me roar..."*

Haggis stuck his head through the doggie door and barked.

"Okay, so I'm a dork. But cut me some slack. I'm feeling pretty good about myself today."

I finished my coffee while Haggis chased a bird around the yard. What a cutie! He'd die if he ever caught one.

I whistled for him. "Come on. Let's go in. Time for Mommy to get dressed. Sheriff John will be here pretty soon."

Not sure how I knew Yazzie was coming. But he was. I knew it. Just like I seemed to know a lot of things lately, without being told. Maybe I'd been feeling the effects of the Sedona vortices.

I'd read a book about it from my store. The theory is that the Earth is an energy grid and there are certain spots where the grids converge. Sedona is supposedly one of them. The area is thought to be home to four major vortices and several other minor ones. Some of them are electrical. Some of them are magnetic. Some of them are electromagnetic. I don't get it. I don't expect you to get it.

All I know is, more spooky stuff has happened to me since I moved here than in my entire life.

And getting back to the point. I knew Sheriff John was coming. And he did, ten minutes later.

I was in the kitchen making him a cup of coffee when he knocked on the screen door. "Come on in, Sheriff. I'm in the kitchen."

John strolled in. "How'd you know it was me?"

"I'm psychic." I smiled and handed him the cup. "Just the way you like it. Two sugars, a dash of cream."

He stared at me suspiciously.

"Houston told me."

He was a tad sarcastic, "You and Houston's ghost talk about my coffee?"

"We talk about a lot of things."

It was then that Houston arrived in a small whirlwind, fluttering my toilé curtains and scattering the newspaper on my table. Haggis yipped and bounced up and down in greeting, begging for Houston to pick him up. Haggis didn't have a good handle on the after-life yet.

John gave him an uneasy stare as I picked up my little guy and tried to calm him down.

"Omigod! He's here," Houston was bursting with excitement. "He's really here." Then he whirled on me, suddenly bitchy as hell, "Why didn't you tell me he was coming?"

"You weren't around."

John frowned. "Around where?"

"Not talking to you."

He gave the room a good once-over. "Then who are you talking to?"

"Houston, of course."

"Yeah, me! John it's me! God how I've missed you! You look wonderful!" Houston was so close, he was nearly in John's lap. But like everyone else in this world, except me of course, John was oblivious.

I think John half believed already, but he was a "show me" kind of guy. "Prove it."

Easy for him to say. "How am I going to do that?"

The smug son of a bitch said, "Ask Houston."

"Okay. Show him," I said to Houston, putting the ball in his court.

"Show him what?" He bounced it right back.

John's right eye began twitching again.

"Well..." I held my coffee mug out to him. "You could levitate this."

"Levitate it?" He snorted. "Levitate it yourself."

"Why not?"

John was just staring at the ceiling now.

Houston pronounced every syllable carefully. "Remember the toilet brush? Remember what a mess I was?"

"Ooh, yeah." Silly me. "Then, what?"

"Oh, oh, I got it," Houston sputtered. "Bay Rum."

"Bay Rum?" I parroted.

John shrugged, "Too easy. Everybody in the county knows I use it. I must get fifty bottles at Christmas."

Houston was sprawled across the table now, propped on his elbows staring at John, his besotted gaze totally adoring. "Isn't he wonderful?"

"Yeah, wonderful."

"What?"

"Oh! Oh! I know! I know!" Houston tried to tap me on the shoulder. "He's got three testicles!"

"He's got what!" My gaze fell to his crotch, my face got fiery hot, and I just died. "No. No. I can't say that. Think of something else."

John's hands dropped instinctively to his privates. He shifted his weight nervously. "This is way too strange." His eyes scoured the room, seeking something he desperately wanted to find, but was afraid to see. "I gotta go." John backed toward the door.

"That's it! Strange!" Houston was nearly yelling in excitement. "Tell him we met when he was looking for a strange man. Tell him, 'I'm no stranger than he is'."

I repeated it quickly, and John stopped dead in his tracks.

John exhaled a ragged breath. "On the day we met, I got a nine-twenty-one on a strange man prowling around the construction site at Cochran's resort. It was a strange man, all right. It was Houston. But I always said he was no stranger than me." John's shoulders started to shake. "Omigod, it's true. He is dead." He dropped his head into his hands.

Great. I made the Sheriff cry. Good job, Tildy.

Houston was beside himself, trying to hug him, but it wasn't working out. "Don't just stand there. Do something."

Like what? "Can I get you another cup of coffee?" I think Houston was hoping for something more Mother Theresa than Martha Stewart, but dead guys can't be picky.

And that was how it came to be that Sheriff John Yazzie was reunited with his long-lost lover, Houston Powers — on one level, anyway. The three of us talked well into the afternoon. John brought Houston up-to-date on his life, both professional and personal. Professional-wise, he was happy as a lark, even if he sometimes felt guilty about how he got the job. His personal life was another matter. He had never stopped loving Houston and he missed him terribly. So, I had two sobbing men on my hands.

Things dried out a little when it was Houston's and my turn to talk. We told John every thing we could think of, including all the evidence I dug up (and I do mean dug up) on the three scumbags.

At one point John's beeper went off. When he came back from calling in, "Couple of things. The Excursion you sank was empty. No sign of your gorilla. Either he made it out or the quicksand got him. We can always hope."

Couldn't happen to a nicer guy. But something told me Donnie was alive and well and planning some spectacular way to off me.

"And our old buddy Cochran called, wanting to know if I'd arrested the vandals who had dug up his golf course. I told him it was pissed-off Indian spirits that did it. That shut the butthead up."

And speaking of buttheads...

Chapter Twenty-Four

...I got to talk to one that very evening.

"Ms. MacNamara, this is Flake. James Flake. Claims adjuster."

Double-O-Butthead. "What can I do for you, Mr. Flake?"

"I'm calling to advise you the insurance company has totaled your car, settled your case, and is forwarding a draft in the agreed amount directly to you."

"Okay." What did he really want? "Thanks for calling."

And then he just couldn't hold it back any more, and all his paranoid frustration poured out. "You think you've gotten away with this. Don't you? Be aware I've had your car hauled to a, shall we say, friendly body shop. If you hit a cow, they'll find out."

Geez, all he needed was the big wart on his nose and a pointed black hat. *I'll get you and your little dog too, my pretty.*

He was nearly cackling, for crying out loud. "There's always evidence left behind, MacNamara. Blood evidence."

It was an epiphany! It was the mother of all epiphanies.

"Blood! Of course! Oh, that's it!" I made kissy noises at the phone. "Oh, thank you, thank you, Mr. Flake. You're such a doll!"

"Doll?" He began to sputter, "But... but..."

I hung up on the jerk and got out the Yellow Pages.

First thing the next morning I started calling body shops. It was a short list after I eliminated the ones that weren't even in business in 1978. Two in Flagstaff, one in Cottonwood, and one in Sedona.

A-1 Auto Body and Towing was my Sedona connection. I stopped by Grace's shop and got enough coffee and chocolate-filled croissants to handle my addiction as well as a bribe for the new owner of the body shop.

Grace was immediately curious about my trip to the body shop, but since she was so squirrelly about the supernatural and didn't know about my resident ghost, I took the easy path and lied. Again.

"Pin-striping for my new wheels," I faked exuberance. "Come on out and have a look at her."

Grace loved the Land Cruiser, said she was practically green with envy, but as I got ready to leave, she stepped up beside me and gave me a hug.

I was surprised, and then she said, "Tildy, honey, be careful. I don't know what to think about this run of bad luck you're having. The ants. The fiasco with Wade Johnson. The breakin. And now, hitting a cow!"

"Yeah," I muttered, "My stars are in the toilet."

Grace shook her head. "I don't buy that, but something is darn sure going on. Just watch your back."

"I will," I promised, feeling incredibly guilty about misleading her. One of these days, I'd have to level with Grace. I didn't want to lose her friendship, but then a true friend doesn't lie, either — unless, of course, your friend happens to ask how she looks in her new swimsuit.

* * * * *

Josephine "Jo" Margolis was six-foot-four and weighed maybe two, two-ten. To quote Jimmy Dean, Jo Margolis was "a mountain" of a woman. Her blonde hair was in a butch cut with spiked red tips that matched her short, blunt fingernails. She wore overalls and "Harley" boots. She was an outrageous flirt. And woe is me, she really, really liked me.

"Yep." Her voice was out of sync with her Russian weightlifter look. It was high and sweet and soft. "My daddy is the one you need to talk to. Back in '78, this was the only body shop in Sedona." She batted her eyes and flexed her biceps.

"And exactly where would I find him?" I smiled weakly. For all my big talk, I was still too square to be comfortable with her hitting on me.

She smiled back. There was chocolate-cream filling smooshed in between her teeth. "He'd be down at Camp Verde under the bridge. Helluva fly-fisher, my daddy. You like it?"

"Like what?" I shifted my weight nervously.

"Fly-fishing," she said slyly. "I could show you how. I could show you real good."

Strains of "Dueling Banjos" floated through my head and the urge to tuck my tail between my legs and run like hell was almost irresistible — especially the tail-tucking part.

"Allergic to fish," I apologized.

She smoothed her hand over her hair and caught me staring at her fingernails, elegantly manicured, yet ringed with grease. "You like red?"

I nodded. "Stunning."

"Keeps the grease from showing so much. Gets in under the nails, ya know." She stepped in close. "I like you a lot, Tildy. A lot. You get me going, sweet thing. You set my heart aflutter. See?" And with that, she grabbed my hand and laid it smack on top of her boulder-hard boob.

I gulped and snatched my hand back. What the hell else could I do, except. "You're nice too, but I'm pitifully straight."

"Oh," she said sadly. "You could give it a try. You might like it."

Or I might not. "No thanks." I turned to get the flock outta there.

She called after me. "Come back sometime, sugar cheeks, and I'll give you a ring job. On the house."

I broke into a run.

* * * * *

Walt Margolis was downright boring next to his, shall we say, "colorful" daughter. He seemed to be a regular guy, in his early seventies, tall and thin. He stood out in the middle of the Verde River in waist-high waders flicking his line. I sloshed out to him, dressed to the nines in the hip-waders I rented at Camp Verde's one and only general store.

Mr. Margolis was a master. His rod danced as the line flew out gracefully over the water. He snapped it back and I watched first in admiration, then in disbelief as the hook headed straight for my head — aw, man — not again — and tangled up in my hair.

He pulled and I went with it.

"Ah, Mr. Margolis?"

He jerked hard and nearly snatched me bald.

"Ow!!"

He finally turned around and saw the hook snarled in my hair. "Oh Lord, Missy. Get over here so I can have a look."

He began to reel me in and I waded out to him, deeper and deeper until I was standing beside him in water up to my waist. He held the rod line loose and "fished" through my matted curls for his hook while my waders filled with ice cold water. I stood still and tried to ignore the fish wiggling around inside my boot.

He got the hook out with only a small clump of hair and apologized profusely. "I'm hard o' hearing, you know. You shouldn't oughta walk up behind a feller like that. I never heard you. Lord, I can't believe I did that." He laughed. "But I reckon you're about the prettiest fish I caught all day."

I rubbed my head and smiled. "No harm done, I guess." At least I wasn't bleeding.

What a ladykiller he must have been in his day. Prettiest fish he'd caught all day, my fanny.

My mom was eighteen years old in 1947, and volunteered at the U.S.O. She fancied herself quite a canary and loved to get up on that stage and warble and shake it some for the troops. That's how she met my dad. Now, don't get me wrong, I love my mom, but she wasn't exactly Mother of the Year. And we shared damn few special moments. But I'll always remember the nights she sang me to sleep. There probably aren't a lot of little girls whose moms dressed up in their old U.S.O. uniforms and marched around the room doing swing numbers.

I'd prop the pillows up and sit there in total ecstasy while she boogied and sang. One in particular that really seemed to fit this occasion went something like this: *I've looked the field over, and lo and behooooold — they're either too young or too old.* Mostly too old. Or too gay. Or too criminally insane. Or too female. Or too dead.

Walt pushed me out of the water up onto the bank, leaving his hand on my rear end a little longer than was necessary. Yep, Jo's woman-chasing was hereditary all right.

Digging the rainbow trout out of my boot, I handed it to him. "Just in case they're not biting."

I sat down on the grass and lifted my legs to about a forty-five degree angle and all the water and gravel and swimming things came pouring out. My sandals and jeans were soaked and sticking to me, but a good detective is not always a dry detective so I forged ahead with my sleuthing.

I talked while Walt straddled my legs and yanked off my boots. "I need to ask if you might possibly have any records left from repairs you did way back in '78?" I handed him one of the over-priced sandwiches from the general store.

He thanked me with a nod and a smile and took a bite. "Nope, I wouldn't have kept anything longer than five years max." Bits of bread and bologna flew out as he talked.

"No records?" I was getting so tired of dead ends.

"No. But, I can tell ya what came in. Ya want the whole year? Or what?"

"Sorry?"

"I got me one of them photogenic minds."

Photogenic? "Oh, you mean photographic. You have a photographic memory?" Glory hallelujah!

And boy, did he!

I sat and listened while he described in painful detail every dent, every scratch, every broken windshield he repaired during January 1978 and exactly how he went about doing it.

At the end of his dissertation, he gave me a bear hug and his hands ended up back on my butt. I didn't even bother to say anything. The old fart was probably just lonesome.

I walked away with basically nothing, only two names I even recognized, and neither of them was exactly what I'd call a desperado.

Big John Yazzie brought in his pickup two days after the New Year. He told Walt he'd been run off the road by a drunk. Walt remembered that his right front fender had a three-quarter-inch-deep dent in the upper quadrant and there was an inch-and-a-half scrape on the bumper.

Grace had hit a deer over the holidays (probably scared the bejeezus out of her) and took her Blazer in with a broken right headlight and a slight bend in the hood.

But Cochran? Huh-uh. Wade Johnson? No such luck.

Another dead end, but I did get to witness first-hand the remarkable performance of Mister Walt Margolis, Memory Guru Extraordinaire for two freakin' hours.

* * * * *

Houston was more depressed than ever. Seeing John wasn't good for him. It really seemed to bring it home that the love of his life was lost to him forever.

He was cranky. That was pretty easy to figure out since light bulbs kept blowing, and the security system kept going off. After the third time, Officer Barnett, minus the leg cast, called the monitoring service himself and told them to forget they ever knew me.

I finally cornered Houston in the pantry and made him calm down and talk it out.

He was completely morose, positive we'd never solve his murder and he'd be stuck in this limbo forever.

Without knowing where it came from, I had this absolutely brilliant ah-ha. "What if I went down to Phoenix and talked Ellen Johnson into rolling over on her ex-husband and exposing the whole land scam scheme?"

He thought about it and maybe even perked up a little. "Yeah? And how would that help my situation?"

"We both think this is all related, right?"

"Yeah."

"Here's the deal. I get her statement implicating all those guys in the reservation land fraud. We bring them all together in one room, just like an Agatha Christy mystery, and hammer them until one of them cracks." I was so excited I could hardly stand it. It was the perfect solution.

He looked at me with a droll expression and said, "Sometimes you're a complete idiot."

Talk about letting the air out of a gal's balloon!

And as if that wasn't harsh enough, he went on, "What the hell are you blithering on about? What do you plan to do? Send them a formal invitation?"

"No need to be so bitchy, Houston," I said gently, then, "That's exactly what I'm going to do — send them a formal invitation."

Let's see: Matilda MacNamara requests the honor of your presence at her home to celebrate the occasion of sending your respective butts to the big house. R.S.V.P.

Black tie only...

Chapter Twenty-Five

...and nothing else — unless you count the black velvet G-string that almost covered his package. Black tie. Black velvet. Valet parking. A formal affair from the get-go.

The place was called Sex Fifth Avenue. Silly me, I wasn't paying close attention and thought Ellen said to meet her at Saks Fifth Avenue.

So, I drove to downtown Scottsdale and, under the neon-lit portico of this lush establishment, turned my car over to the valet, a most charming young man in a silk muscle-shirt and a pair of skin-tight leather pants. Should have been my first clue, right? That and the big banner out front declaring it was "Ladies' Night."

It took a few minutes for my eyes to adjust to the darkness inside. But once they did, I knew I wasn't in Kansas anymore, Toto.

Marble and chrome, and lasers slashing through the darkness, punctuated by the thump and squeal of Euro-tech music. Every table was filled and every chair was taken by women. Women of every race and age. College girls, working girls, country-club women, and grandmas. And every one of them was a crazed, screaming idiot.

The maitre'd made Donnie look like a wimp. He was an incredibly handsome black man with a shaved head. His pecs and biceps were barely contained under the black tee-shirt with the "Sex Fifth Avenue" logo plastered across the front.

He smiled and his one gold tooth glittered as a laser bounced off it. "Do you have a reservation, Miss?"

Miss? Ohmigod. I was in love.

"Reservation? I don't know. I'm here to meet Ellen Johnson." He was so good-looking it was hard not to be coy.

He nodded and his smile widened. "Oh, sure. My girl, Ellie. She's right over there."

I followed his pointing finger to a table right up front next to the stage where Ellen Johnson was at the mercy of a well-endowed energetic lap-dancer thrusting his equipment in her face. She loved it. Are we surprised?

Like I said before, the dancer was sort of wearing a black bow tie and a black velvet G-string, but for all intents and purposes he was buck naked. Ellen kept stuffing bills in his G-string like it was the overnight deposit slot at the bank.

There was no sense even trying to talk to her until she'd had her fill of the Hispanic stud whose nose was now between her enormous breasts. I might as well have a drink, enjoy the view and try not to die of embarrassment. I walked over to Ellen's table just as her lap dance was over.

She saw me, jumped up and gave me a quick hug. "Oh, Tildy, I'm glad to see you. You were so kind to take care of me that night and I never got the chance to repay you. I decided to treat you to a nice little evening out."

She ordered two drinks from a haggard cocktail waitress and shoved one across to me. The lights came up on stage and Ellen touched my arm. "Wait 'til you get a load of these guys. They'll rock your boat."

The music kicked in and the show began. As I sank slowly in my chair, a dozen glistening male bodies burst onto the stage and began to wriggle and gyrate and...

"Take it off, baby," Ellen brayed and jumped up onto the stage.

The crowd went wild. And it was totally infectious. Easy to lose yourself and your mind when everybody around you is screaming and jumping up and down and getting into it. Mob mentality. It was a theory Andrew the Anus always subscribed to, although I don't think he ever applied it to male strippers.

I relaxed and went with the flow. Had some drinks, got ripped, and before long I was making a few night deposits of my own.

The club called a taxi to take us back to Ellen's since neither of us was in any shape to drive.

Ellen insisted I stay the night, and so began the slumber party from Hell.

I gotta hand it to her. The woman could hold her liquor. She had twice as many martinis as I did and the bitch was still upright. I, on the other hand, was on my knees puking in the guest toilet, while Ellen whipped up a mean cheese omelet in the kitchen. The smell nearly killed me. I declined the eggs, but took the coffee, and after a while I began to feel better.

I sat out on the elegant patio while Ellen and her huge boobs went for a late-night swim, nude of course. She was a great floater, even if mascara was running all over her face.

It was one in the morning and still sweltering. The monsoons had arrived in force and the humidity was murder. Ellen toweled off, then went over and switched on a pump which "misted" the pool area. In my diminished state, it took a few minutes to realize it wasn't raining, it was only a malfunctioning spray nozzle dripping on top of my head.

Chinese water torture.

Ellen was in manic mode, ping-ponging from oversexed party girl to someone in serious need of a good dose of Lithium. There was a lot of hurt and humiliation hiding behind that facade of silicone and mascara. After all those years, she still carried a red-hot poker inside her, just waiting for Wade to come around so she could poke it in his eye — or lower.

"I really, really liked being a Senator's wife, Tildy. Old Wade, I could take or leave, but I loved the life — the parties, the respect, the perks. The bastard just took it all away, for no reason at all. Hell, I coulda cared less about him and his little interns. Why'd he have to go and divorce me, anyhow? Just threw me out like an old hanging chad." She broke down and cried like a kid. I took the opportunity to scoot my chair out from under the deluge, then leaned over and put my arm around her.

She responded to that small kindness with an enormous hunger, grabbing me and holding me against her, sobbing uncontrollably. Poor Ellen, used and abused and thrown out. Must be some heavy shit in her karma, because I was getting ready to use her again.

"Ellen?"

She sniffed and blew her nose on the towel, causing it to slip down off her breasts. I had to concentrate on keeping my gaze above her neck. "After all these years, how would you like to exact your pound of flesh from the bastard?"

She blinked, "You mean Wade?"

I nodded.

"Pound of flesh, huh? Yeah. I'd like it a lot. You know where I'd take it from?" She ground her fist into her palm.

I shook my head and eased back in the chair. Had I created a monster?

It was an evil smile. "Cut off his dick."

I cringed.

She added, "Of course, to make up a pound, I'd have to take his balls, too. What did you have in mind?"

So I told her about my crusade against Johnson and his cronies, and of my dream that she would testify against him.

When I was done telling her, there was a murderous light in her eye. "Have I got a deal for you! All I ask in return is when you bring him down, put in a good word for me over at ABC. I always wanted Barbara Walters to ask me what kind of tree I'd be."

"Tree?" She'd kinda lost me there.

"I'd be a palm tree so I could have *biiig* coconuts." She cupped her hands under her coconuts and the towel fell away completely. "Come with me." She stood and padded nude into the house.

I followed behind thinking there was something to be admired about her openness, both spiritual and physical. She'd just unloaded the weight of her world onto a total stranger, and was now parading around starkers without a thought to age, droop or cellulite. Not me, not in a million years. And believe me, it's a humanitarian gesture.

We sat at the breakfast bar and drank coffee until dawn, making our plan, then, on two hours sleep, we went out and got some breakfast at The Pancake House on Camelback and Scottsdale. By that time the cooking eggs smelled terrific.

We hit the bank at ten and liberated Ellen's illegal cassette recordings of Wade and Attanasio, Wade and Cochran, Wade and Big John. There were even a few X-rated — woo-woo! — tapes of Wade and a hooker named Bambi.

Thank you, Ellen Johnson, my hero. Nothing like a paranoid, bitter, publicity-hungry bitch out for revenge to turn your case around.

You know what they say: Hell hath no fury like...

Chapter Twenty-Six

...a gaggle of senior citizens banned from having sex in the Sun City clubhouse pool.

"I tell you, girl, it's a sight." Mrs. Powers craned her neck to see past the picketing seniors and the Sheriff's "posse" to the TV crews taping the protest. "You see that man over there, the one with the walker?"

"Mmm, the one with the sign that says, 'If God wanted us to stop screwing, he wouldn't have invented Viagra?'"

"That's him, Don Juan Peterson. He's the one got interviewed by Maria Shriver, you know. He was taking on the local girls two at a time. Lord-a-mercy, they had to call an ambulance for Sofie Antonelli. She was in such a swoon when he got done with her." Mrs. Powers fanned herself with her hankie. "You ever watch that Maria Shriver? She could use a few pounds. Don't you think?" Universal, isn't it. All us plump girls think Maria Shriver could use a few pounds; and Mrs. Powers was definitely one of "us plump girls."

I considered the elderly gentleman shuffling around the pool with the other picketers. Hard to imagine him in a raucous sex orgy. But even the networks knew public sex was an issue at "Sin City."

Over by the pool, one of the geriatric babes went ballistic and tore off her shirt, screaming: "Give us liberty, or give us death." and jumped into the pool. Two of Sheriff Joe's auxiliary jumped in after her and all hell broke loose.

A half-dozen more Sun City denizens went in and it became a dunking and splashing contest between the deputies and the seniors — the old dudes were winning. The women started chanting: "Free sex. Free sex. Free sex."

The TV crews jockeyed for position. One cameraman got too near the edge, and Don Juan bumped him with his walker, knocking both the camera and the cameraman into the deep end.

It was all pretty exciting. Who knew Sun City was such a hotbed of political unrest and randy old folks? I nearly forgot why I was there in the first place.

To brighten Houston's mood and help lift him out of his depression, I promised to visit his mother, check on her and deliver a very specific message. I'd been dreading it all day, but now that I saw what a rolling party it was around there, I might just come down on a regular basis.

I'd found Mrs. Powers poolside, along with about half the population of the entire state, watching the spectacle unfold. She was plump and sweet and dressed like a normal person (everything my mom never was). She was Richie's mom from *Happy Days*. I liked her immediately.

When I told her I had a message from Houston, she didn't even blink, just took it in stride like she'd been expecting to hear from him. "Let's go on over to my place, honey. He'll be needing his notebook. I can't imagine how he's managed without it all this time."

Present tense. She spoke of him in present tense. Oh, swell. Houston, I really, really hate you.

Her two-bedroom condo was bright and pleasant, done in pastels. My guess was her life's mission was to crochet doilies. If there was one doily, there were a hundred. Doilies everywhere, every size, every shape, every color in the rainbow. Never been a big doily fan myself, but to each his own.

She went into the bedroom and brought out an old dog-eared scrapbook and a big brown envelope. "My son is a brilliant man." She moved a doily-in-progress aside and sat down beside me on the sofa. Mrs. Powers flipped open the book and shoved it under my nose. I took it and politely began to go through page after page of clippings, photographs, awards — every word ever written by or about Houston Powers. And there was a lot. How the hell was I going to tell her? Damn him for making me promise.

"Mrs. Powers?"

"Call me Minnie."

Gulp.

"Minnie, Houston's dead, dear. He died twenty-five years ago in a car accident. I'm a psychic and he sent you a message through me. He wants you to know how much he loves you. How much it meant that you always accepted, never condemned or questioned. And that his spirit is with you. Always."

Her eyes misted up and I thought for a minute I might lose her in a flurry of grief, but she held it together and smiled. "I know, dear. Houston is such a good boy, I knew he'd send a message." Then she winked. "What the hell do you think took him so long? You tell him we'll see each other again, not too soon, I hope."

Heaving a big sigh of relief, I couldn't help but marvel at her calm acceptance. What I told her wasn't news, it was just a reiteration of what she'd known all along.

"He's asked me to check up on you every once in a while, make sure you're all right."

"Such a good boy." Minnie smiled.

"Would that be okay?"

"Well, I suppose. But I don't need a bloody thing, dear. I sunk a wad into AOL at its start-up and got out at the top. I'm set for life. You need anything?"

"No, I got out at the top, too. The top of my ex-husband's earning power."

We both got a good laugh out of that, and then we got a good laugh out of the parade of naked geriatrics prancing down the street — signs (and everything else, for that matter) waving in the breeze. Anybody bring sun screen?

"Oh my, Tildy, there's a lot of exposed skin out there that would have best been left hidden." She got up, closed the shutters and brought my attention back to the scrapbook.

"Look, dear. Here's Houston's prizewinner." The yellowed, magazine page with Houston's byline was the same article on Sasha the Guerilla Terrorist I'd read back when I was doing my computer research.

"You're very proud of him, aren't you?" I said.

"Well, who wouldn't be? Just look at this. He risked his life infiltrating their secret society. Why, it was all because of my Houston the gang was brought down. They were all tried and convicted, too. Too bad that Sasha person escaped punishment. What a piece of work, that one. You know the story, right?"

Not only did I know, I could almost recite it. How Sasha and the Fighters for Liberated Peoples reigned in terror during the late sixties and early seventies with bank robberies, assaults on public buildings, kidnappings and bombings. Their crowning glory came in 1970 when they fire-bombed the World News Magazine Building. Three security guards and five FLP terrorists died that night. Houston had, at great personal risk, gathered enough evidence against them and their leader Sasha for the authorities to make a case. They were hunted down like the animals they were, jailed, tried, convicted and imprisoned. The only fly in the ointment of justice was when Sasha escaped during a work detail and was never heard from again. Houston deserved all the awards and recognition heaped on him. The series was his *piece de resistance.*

And Minnie had every right to bust her buttons.

I closed the scrapbook and picked up my handbag. "Minnie, it's a long drive back to Sedona and I better get going."

As I stood up, she handed me the big brown envelope.

"This is Houston's notebook, Tildy. He left it in his rental car. When the police found the car, they gave everything to me. See he gets it, will you? He needs it."

When my fingers closed over the envelope, I was zapped by a jolt of near-electrical current. Wow. There was something really important here, but just out of reach of my psychic abilities. A vision had tried to get through, but just like before, I short-circuited. Maybe if I went over the notebook with Houston, it would come in more clearly the next time.

I drove back up I-17 grinning like a Cheshire cat.

Things were looking up. I'd done my duty to Houston's mom and while the anticipation of it was total stress, the actuality was kind of fun. My solicitation of Ellen's testimony worked out better than I could have wished. Not only did she agree to testify in court that her husband had browbeat her into helping them cover their trail with phantom deeds, she presented me with tangible evidence that would be the Elmer's I planned to use to glue my case together.

You gotta know I was practically preening. Next, John, Houston, and I would set our trap for ol' Brer Rabbit and his pals, lure them in with a good old-fashioned tar baby. And that tar baby would be me. Oh, yeah.

Zip-a-dee-doo-dah, zip-a-dee-ay. My oh my...

Chapter Twenty-Seven

"...we're gonna put 'em away." John Yazzie promised Houston sincerely.

Actually, he was just promising the corner of the living room. Houston was sitting beside him on the couch, but I didn't want to burst his bubble.

Haggis cocked his head to one side and looked at John like — there's nobody over there, fool. He kept running over and trying to sit in Houston's "lap" as if to say: Here he is. Hey, John, over here.

I picked up Haggis, did the ear-scratch thing he loves so much and sang to him: "*Zip-a-dee-do-dah. Zip-a-dee-ay.*" It wasn't one of his favorites, he's partial to the Oscar Meyer Wiener Song. But I was in a zip-a-dee-doo-dah mood, positive we were making big-time progress now and we'd have this whole thing sewed up in a couple of days.

"Good work, Tildy," Houston beamed proudly. "Looks like we make a good team. I'll be knocking on the pearly gates any time now."

"I'll miss you," I said.

"What?" John asked.

"Houston. I'll miss Houston when he's not hanging around here any more."

"Oh." John got up from the sofa and knelt in front of the corner. "Good night, good night! Parting is such sweet sorrow."

"Uh, John?"

He looked around, and I jerked my head toward the sofa.

He changed knees and flipped around, "Good night, sweet prince, and flights of angels sing thee to thy rest."

I got all misty. "That's so sweet."

Houston floated over and kissed him on the cheek. Now, I know Houston always said no one but me could see him or hear him or feel him. But the light shining in John's eyes made me think otherwise.

Houston twirled in the air and laughed out loud. "Oh, honey, I'm almost home."

* * * * *

Yazzie had come by the morning after I got back from Phoenix to take me with him to Flagstaff. Northern Arizona University's audiovisual lab had a special machine that would treat our fragile tapes with T.L.C. while copying it to CD.

Sheriff John agreed to participate in our "sting" operation providing the tapes were as incriminating as Ellen had promised. So, not only would I get the goons off my back when they tossed them in the hoosgow (please don't think I'm being a bitch) but I'd get good old Houston off my back, too.

My life would be mine again, back to normal. No ghosts serenading me in the middle of the night. No more interviewing scumbags. No more dodging bullets of senile mobsters. No more midnight-killer toilet-brush incidents. No more playing bumper cars with steely-eyed hit men. Just me and Haggis and my friends and the bookstore and normalcy. I could hardly wait.

We took 89-A, the back way, to Flagstaff through mountains and a dark green sea of trees. I opened the envelope Ellen gave me.

"How many are there?" John kept his eyes on the serpentine road ahead.

"Four," I said nonchalantly. "One with Cochran, one with Attanasio, one we probably won't use — unless you're into heavy breathing...."

He smiled. So handsome. You think he'd ever consider converting?

"...and one with a fella name John Yazzie Senior."

His smiled died. "Dammit. I hoped his name wouldn't come up. Don't want to arrest my own father. But guess I knew all along if we opened this can of worms, all the worms would wiggle out."

"How can you say that about him? He's not a worm. He's wonderful. John, whatever he did, he did for the tribe. He did it for you."

He was unyielding. "Motive is no excuse for breaking the law. Conspiracy is conspiracy. I took an oath. My word is a covenant with the people of this county. I can't just throw evidence away. I have to deal with it."

I looked at him a long time, at the set of his jaw, the hard grip he had on the steering wheel. Then I noticed his right eye was twitching again.

"Deal with what?" I rolled down the window and threw out the tape. It spun over the railing and plummeted into the deep ravine below. It was out of sight when John slammed on the brakes and pulled over to the side.

"What the hell do you call that?" he demanded, fire in his eyes.

"Littering? What's the fine?" I tried to smile. What I did scared the hell out of me. I mean, after all, it really was evidence. What if I'd read him wrong? What if his feelings for his father weren't there? What if he really would have the old man hauled in? What if he had me hauled in?

But, for once, my intuition hit a bull's eye.

He grimaced and reached across to open the glove box. "This'll cost you."

I was suddenly very unsure again. What was he after? Gun? Cuffs?

No. His ticket book. He opened it and began to write. What the man handed me was a citation for littering.

"This will cost you five hundred bucks, Tildy. But," he smiled, "maybe we could work out some community service."

I slid over and gave him a kiss on the cheek.

"You're my kind of guy, Little John."

He shifted into drive, checked his rearview mirror, and pulled back out onto the road, smiling. "There are lots worse things to be."

* * * * *

The tapes proved to be everything we'd hoped for and more. I'd secretly hoped some little something might slip out about Houston on one of the tapes that would make our manhunt unnecessary — like maybe Joe Attanasio would mention his plan to murder the snoopy reporter, or maybe Wade, or even Cochran. But the timeline was off. The land scam was perpetrated against the Navajo tribe and the Bureau of Land Management in the first half of the seventies when the Navajo-Hopi Land Settlement Act drew new boundaries between the Hopis and the Navajos. Our guys were tied in with other Congressmen and energy interests whose sole intent was to walk off with mineral and water rights. Vast quantities of oil, uranium and coal were at stake, as well as valuable land for commercial development. Which brings us back to Attanasio, Wade Johnson, and Ted Cochran. Houston wasn't murdered until 1978.

Yazzie was raring to go. After listening to Ellen's tapes, as well as the taped conversation with Big John at the rodeo, and reviewing all the material I'd brought back from Flagstaff, he knew he'd get them — if not for Houston's murder (which we had yet to prove), then at least for screwing over the Navajo Nation.

And something else Sheriff John knew after all this input — his father wasn't the sell-out he thought. Big John always had the best interest of the tribe at heart. He'd been duped, then blackmailed into keeping quiet about it.

All the way back from Flagstaff, John talked about the case. "I can't wait for these low-down dirty two-faced snakes to get a good look at the inside of my jail."

And he talked about his dad. "Guess I need to go see the old man and let him know I finally understand. Maybe we'll be able to tear down that wall I put between us."

And he talked about Houston. "We solve this murder, we're taking him home. To rest. He loved Cathedral Rock. We always went there to watch the sun set. It was our spot."

I didn't know what to say so I didn't say anything. You may want to write that down on your calendar — that I kept my mouth shut, it being such a rare occasion and all.

He went on, "Will you come, Tildy? He'd probably want you there, too, you know, when I scatter his ashes."

"Of course." If we ever found the body, but no sense in bringing that up then.

He dropped me off at the house, but didn't come in. There was a lot to do in preparation for our sting. He had to set up a video surveillance at the house — said he'd do it later, and for me to tell Houston he'd "see" him then. But first he had to see a judge about some warrants and make arrangements with Chief Parrish for the extra manpower to cover the operation.

I didn't have to be psychic to know what kind of response he'd get from Bill Parrish: "Her again?!"

Yep, looked like Tildy's house was the center of the social scene for the next twenty-four hours. John and his surveillance crew setting up, Bill and his cranky officers lying in wait, Joe Attanasio and his sidekick Donnie (oh shit), Wade Johnson, Ted Cochran — the list just kept on growing.

What the hell, the more the merrier. May as well go stand out in the road, wave my arms and do my carnival barker routine: "Ladies and Gentlemen, Boys and Girls, come one. Come all. You'll be amazed. You'll be arrested. You'll be..."

Chapter Twenty-Eight

"...out of your freakin' mind?" Chloe shook her head in disbelief. "They've already tried to kill you twice. They say third time's the charm."

"Or," I smiled grimly. "Three strikes and you're out."

Chloe, Joaquin, and I were running ourselves ragged at the store, busier than a one-legged man at a polka contest. I'd completely forgotten it was the day Madame Simone, Queen of the Tarot, and Prince Gregor were appearing at the Spirit of the Vortex. She was signing her new book and giving readings — the same day John Yazzie was transforming my place into the bridge of the Enterprise. I was watching in fascination as the technical surveillance crew turned the house into a technological marvel, covering their tracks so completely, even I couldn't tell where they put all their spy stuff.

That's when the phone rang and Chloe's frantic voice cried, "Where are you? The phone's ringing off the hook. So many people coming in and out, we need a swinging door. The register already needs emptying. I'm losing my mind. Joaquin's losing his smile. We need you!"

"Uh. I forgot." Another senior moment. "I'll be right down."

*****

Haggis and I jumped in the car and drove straight there. In the middle of our three-ring circus of writing up book sales, juggling appointments for Madame Simone and Gregor, and pulling women off Joaquin, I managed to fill in Chloe on our master plan for catching the culprits. Like I said before, she thought I'd gone completely around the bend, but we were so busy she didn't have time to scold me much.

Madame Simone was world-famous. Her specialty was finding lost things. Maybe she could find Houston's grave.

She worked with Prince Gregor, a monkey she insisted was the reincarnation of Richard Nixon, who pulled cards for her readings. Her books were always bestsellers, and when she made a personal appearance people came from everywhere to be read.

She was a mysterious lady from Savannah who always dressed in flowing black chiffon and wore enormous hats with nearly opaque veils. No one (that I know of) had ever seen her face, except maybe for Prince Gregor. He was dressed in a miniature three-piece suit with a power tie, and had a habit of making a "V" for victory with both tiny hands.

Simone was just finishing up a session where she located a lost recipe for Ellie Jean from the café nearby. It was the recipe for Ellie Jean's grandma's famous peach cobbler and Simone said that Buffalo Bill stole it to use in his steak house across the street. Ellie Jean stomped out in a huff muttering something about vigilante justice.

I had Chloe call Buffalo Bill's to give him a head's up. After all, Sedona was my home town now and I had no desire to see a hanging on Main Street.

It was about that time that Prince Gregor took a sudden bodacious liking to Haggis, jumped on his back and began — dear Lord — humping him. Haggis yelped and spun in a circle trying to dislodge the amorous simian.

"Hey!" I yanked Gregor off Haggis' back. "Stop that, you little pervert. He's just a baby."

Haggis took shelter between my legs, barking like crazy, reading Gregor the riot act. Gregor was pissed, talk about your "coitus interuptus," and showed it by biting me on the hand. I flung him away with a screech. He sailed straight across the room, landing right on top of Simone's head, knocking off the hat.

Simone dove off the chair, scrabbling around on her hands and knees for the hat. She grabbed it, but before she could get it back on, she conked her head on the table leg and collapsed in a heap on the floor.

It was pandemonium. Gregor was rolling around on the floor, holding himself, shrieking dramatically like he was in the throes of death.

Everyone stampeded over to the reading table where Simone lay half-senseless to get a look at her face. It was like a bag of cash fell off the truck, a total free-for-all — folks knocking each other aside, books falling off the shelves, displays toppling — until the vultures finally formed a circle around her, and gasped as one: *Look at that! She's a man!!*

What can I say? "She" was, with a most handsome five o'clock shadow creeping across "her" jaw and everything. The sound of dozens of snapping shutters brought Simone around and all the poor thing could do was grab the hat for cover.

Ah, yes, another fine summer day at Spirit of the Vortex Book Store.

Chloe, Joaquin and I took pity, and while Joaquin hustled the chattering patrons out of the store, Chloe and I helped "Monsieur" Simone to his/her feet and into the office, then closed the door.

Chloe went out, returning after a couple of minutes with Prince Gregor whom she found buried beneath the cushions in the reading nook. He jumped into Simone's lap and sat there trembling and whimpering. Simone stroked him comfortingly while Haggis backed into a corner under the desk, growling.

Simone didn't even bother with the hat. He just raised his eyes to mine and said, "It's a tough job, but somebody's gotta do it."

I laughed out loud.

Chloe was more serious. "What are you going to do? I mean, they saw."

"Who knows. Maybe the publicity will do more good than harm." He shrugged. "And if not, well, c'est la vie. I can always go back to the phone lines."

"Psychic hot lines?" Chloe asked.

"Not quite. Just 'hot lines'," he said with a wink. "I used to do phone sex."

"Well, Simone," I tried to be philosophical about the whole thing. "A girl's gotta do what a girl's gotta do."

"You said it, cookie." He flopped the hat back on his head. "But call me Simon. And while I'm at it, come here, girl." He crooked his finger at me.

"What?" I looked at Chloe. She shrugged.

"Just come here," he said again, "and let me have a look at your hand."

I took a couple of reluctant steps and hesitantly gave him my hand, the one with the teeth marks.

"Sorry about that," Simon rubbed the spot with his thumb. "At least he didn't break the skin."

I glared at Prince Gregor, who bared his teeth and hissed. "You ever think maybe he's the reincarnation of Hannibal Lecter?" I asked.

Simon didn't answer. He was frowning now and his grip had tightened considerably. I wanted to pull away, but something kept me from doing it.

"What you seek lies in the orchard," he intoned.

"Big wow, Sherlock," I said. "Even I know that. Hell, I already dug up over half of it. Could you be more specific?"

"Thirty paces south of Matilda's heart." He said it like it was the answer to the meaning of life in the Universe.

Me? I didn't know any more than when he started with this fiasco. "Well, thanks a lot, Nostradamus." I took my hand back. "Keep in touch."

"There's danger in the orchard, Tildy. Two graves. One old. One new. His and yours."

A chill rattled along my spine. "Do you know who killed him? We really need to know."

He shook his head. "Only that the one who killed him is coming for you."

Swell. Nothing like a good death prophecy to start your day off right.

The rest of the afternoon went pretty smooth considering what had happened during the morning.

There were a couple of exciting moments when a reporter from the *Red Rock News* came by for an interview. Simon was open and honest and explained how he'd never been accepted as a mystic until he "became" Madame Simone, and that he honestly believed his gift was too important to waste, so he'd done what he felt he had to do. The interview was pretty short. You should have seen the look on the reporter's face when Gregor started humping his leg. The poor guy jumped to his feet, babbled something about leaving his iron on and ran out.

Bill Parrish made a special trip over to see "what the hell kind of zoo" I was running to create such havoc in his town. It seemed there was a crowd-management problem on the sidewalk in front of my store. And then he'd had to go over to Buffalo Bill's to talk Ellie Jean out of chasing off Bill's customers by parading up and down the sidewalk with a sign that read, "Pilfered Cobbler Sold Here."

At six, Simon packed up and got ready to leave. He was driving down to Phoenix, then flying out to New York that very night to do the *Today* show the next morning. His agent had called after the "unveiling" and said the story was all over the news and Katie Couric wanted the exclusive. Simon said he planned to get right to work on his next book, an autobiography — probably be a best-seller.

Looked like things might work out for him after all.

He even thanked me. What do you think about that?

Before he walked out, he reminded me again, "Take care, death walks at your side."

"Get outta here, you Vincent Price wannabe." I gave him and the friggin' monkey a good-natured shove out the door. "Like I need that."

"So long. I'll give you a call when my next book comes out, give you first shot at signing dates." He called through the closing door, "Take care, and don't forget my warning."

I locked the door and reached for the shade, noticing that damn monkey giving me the victory sign over Simon's shoulder. *I am not a crook.*

I pulled down the shade and flipped the sign to "closed," muttering under my breath, "From ghoulies and ghosties and long-leggety beasties and things that go bump in the night, Good Lord, deliver us!"

It was just for good measure, the prayer. I wasn't really frightened of ghoulies, or ghosties or long-leggety beasties, not much anyway. I was pretty cool with things that go bump in the night. Mostly, I was worried about things that go bump...

Chapter Twenty-Nine

...on my head. Solid things, like Donnie's fist. Or ephemeral things like the guilty weight of Houston's misery.

Speaking of Houston's misery, I was surprised to find him in a funk.

"What's wrong with you?" The kitchen was freezing. I'd had to put on a coat in July. So cold, I was thinking of making a fire in my stone pizza oven. "You're almost done with all this. Your season in Hell is nearly finished. You should be on top of the world!"

He wouldn't look at me when he said, "Guess I'm just nervous about tomorrow. You sure it'll be alright?"

"No," I laughed anxiously. "I got a pretty good case of the jitters myself." And to prove it, I ate half a German chocolate cake, which I guess I should have skipped. It rolled around in my stomach way past bedtime.

* * * * *

I am so friggin' scared I can't think straight. My car fishtails around the bend. The beams of my headlights careen wildly over the twisting roadway. Darkness surrounds me. Grasping skeletal fingers claw at the car, ripping shrieking metal away in strips. No, not fingers. Branches. Spiny branches whipping in the wind. The car starts to disintegrate around me. The cold night air blasts across my face. The tires squeal as I flee. Flee from what? I look in the rearview mirror to see —

Eyes. Glowing, malevolent eyes growing closer and closer. A demon swooping down to devour my very soul. No, not eyes. Not a demon. Lights. Headlights. A car, coming fast, coming too fast to escape.

And suddenly my car is gone and I'm rolling, tumbling over the asphalt. I get up and stumble, desperately trying to run. My legs won't move. I turn and the lights are everywhere, blinding me. Now it's too late and I cry out. Pain, such horrible pain. Blackness. At first there's nothing. No light. No sound. Nothing, then I hear —

- scraping. Metal against what? Stone? As my eyes focus I become aware of trees surrounding me. Dark menacing trees shrouded in a swirling mist, and something else. A dim shadow. Someone digging? Digging what?

And now, I'm dropping, falling down, down. A grave. Oh shit! A grave! Moist dirt is dumped on my face. In my mouth, in my eyes. I can't scream. I can't breathe.

A clap of thunder. A crack of lightning. The sky let loose and hail hammered the roof. I jerked awake gasping, fighting my way out of the damp, tangled sheets. Haggis licked my face, whimpering, worried.

The dream had been so vivid this time, I was a little worried myself.

"Sorry, Tildy, I'm so sorry. I didn't mean to. I tried to stop it, but it just got away from me." Houston hiccuped, sobbing uncontrollably. "I can't... can't..."

I crawled to the foot of the bed and sat next to him. I'd seen him hurt, angry, happy, proud, in love, sad — but never like that — never completely hysterical.

My first instinct was to put my arms around him, but I wound up hugging myself. "Oh, honey, what's the matter?"

"I'm scared, Tildy. Scared about the sting." Sobs punctuated his words. "Scared for you if you do it. Scared for me if you don't. You think I want to see you end up like me?"

"You think I might?"

"It's dangerous." Always a master of understatement. "It could blow apart so fast you wouldn't have time to duck. They're bad men, Tildy. They'd kill you in a heartbeat." His tears eased, his sobs lessened. "No." His voice became stronger and more confident. "I'm not willing to risk it. And that's that."

"Do you think I don't know the risk?" Suddenly I was angry. Lack of sleep, blood-curdling nightmares and putting my life at risk tends to do that to me. "Just who do you think you are, anyway? It's my ass, and if I'm willing to put it on the line for you, that's my business."

He shook his head. "My business, too."

"This is my gift to you, Houston. You've already given me so much. It's all I can do for you. Please, don't reject it."

"Forget it. You're not doing it. Call John. Tell him it's off."

I was spitting mad and more than a little hurt. "You get me all worked up, make me believe I'm doing something worthwhile and then you yank the rug out from under me. What the hell kind of friend are you?"

"The kind that gives up eternity for you, Tildy."

Well that took the wind out of my sails. "Oh. That kind."

He was becoming literally more transparent. "Call John. Tell him it's off. Do it, Tildy." And he vanished.

The room temperature rose twenty-five degrees, so I took off my sweatshirt and socks and crawled back between the sheets. But I couldn't go back to sleep, and I didn't call John.

* * * * *

I finally gave up around four-thirty in the morning, made some white chocolate latte, then carried it out on the back porch seeking comfort and tranquility for my soul.

But the storm from the night before had veiled the canyon in fog. It slithered up the bank from the creek, alive and menacing, transforming my orchard into the spectral graveyard of my nightmare.

Just swell.

And then the blood-red sun pierced the mist like a flaming sword. Despite my bravado with Simon, I couldn't help but shudder, remembering his warning. And I had to admit, I was spooked.

The best way to deal with things unseen is to bring them into the realm of reality. My fears would be history when I confronted them head on with my old stand-by "Pros and Cons" list. What better way to make a decision?

I wrote: THE STING (only mine was minus Redford and Newman, of course — dammit), then I made two columns labeled: PROS and CONS.

Under PROS, I wrote the number one, then, *For Houston.* And two, *For Justice.* Finally, three, *For Me.* For who I am right now. Today. This minute.

Under CONS. Number One (seemed pretty obvious to me), *I could get killed.* Number Two. *I could get killed.* And most importantly, Number Three, *I could get killed.*

Okay, I made my list. It didn't change a thing. I still didn't have a clue if I should go ahead with the planned bust or not.

I needed some advice and the only stable person in my life without a vested interest in the matter (like John, for instance) was Grace.

I called her and woke her up, told her I was in trouble and begged her to come over for breakfast.

A friend in need may be a friend indeed, but in my book (and this *is* my book), the friend who rides in with the cavalry is the real champ.

* * * * *

She showed up with bloodshot eyes, bad hair (oh thank you, God, she's not perfect after all), and a shoulder to cry on.

"You look terrible," she said between bites of chocolate-chip pancakes.

"Thanks," I said. "You're so kind to mention it."

She chewed the last bite, carried the plate to the sink, poured another cup of coffee and sat down at the table, fiddling with the ruffled edge of the placemat. "Okay, lady. Let's hear it. What's up?"

I heaved a really big sigh, pulled my dog-eared nine-by-twelve envelope out of the drawer and laid it in front of her.

"I've taken up this new hobby," I said.

She stared at me like I had at least three heads, "You called me at five in the morning to talk about your hobby?"

"Well, kind of."

"What hobby?" She was cranky all right.

"Sleuthing," I said brightly. "I'm investigating the twenty-five-year-old murder of a reporter named Houston Powers." I opened the envelope and spilled the contents in front of her: all my Bolles research, copies of the bogus land deeds, the police report of Houston's disappearance, Houston's *World News Magazine* series on Sasha, Houston's notebook, and my own scribbled notes.

"This is your... your... did you say — hobby?" Her eyes flicked over the pages with some alarm. "Tildy, what is this?"

I launched into it, afraid if I didn't just blurt it all out at once, she'd have the chance to get up and leave. I didn't stop until I got to the night before when Houston made it perfectly clear he didn't want me anywhere near Attanasio and the others.

Grace never said a word during the entire story. She just sat there, unmoving, her eyes glued to the papers strewn across the table. After a minute the silence was kind of unnerving.

"Grace?"

She finally looked up at me. Her color was off and her gaze guarded. Yep, she thought I was crackers all right. "Ghosts, Tildy?"

"I'm not crazy, Grace. It's true, every word. How else would I know all this?" I shoved the articles under her nose. "It's real. I swear."

Her eyes flew over the newsprint on Bolles and the Fighters for Liberated Peoples, then I took her hand and pulled her along to the living room, pointing out all the surveillance equipment. "See?"

We went back to the kitchen and I let her digest it, so to speak.

I thought she still looked a little pale. "Wow. What a story, Tildy. Let's say I believe you, not about the ghost, of course, but the rest — yeah. I guess I can buy that. What in heck do you think you're doing?"

Her reaction threw me off. "What do you mean?"

"It's too dangerous." Good old Grace, always cutting to bottom line.

"So that's a 'no.' I shouldn't do it."

"That's a no." She heaved a big sigh. "But if there was a soul in limbo, the truly heroic thing would be to save him. *If* there was a ghost."

If there was a soul in limbo who'd saved the world from a merciless terrorist, he deserved more than an eternity in purgatory. "Yeah," I said softly, "*If.*"

Grace finished her thought. "The smart move is to back off, Tildy, and let the professionals do their thing. And I pray to God you play it smart. Play it safe." She smiled and shrugged. "But I know you, darlin'. You never play it safe. You have this shining decency and incredible courage that won't allow you to stand by and let someone this evil walk away. It's just not you, kid. So I know, no matter what I say to you, you'll do the ethical thing and help put these bastards away."

I cleared my throat. "So that's a 'yes.'"

* * * * *

Grace hung around and kept me company for a couple of hours until Sheriff John showed up, then left to open her shop.

He handed me the script we'd use to entrap the evil trio. It read like a Mike Hammer novel. Wow! I could get into this. All I needed was a trench coat, slut-red lipstick and a black fedora. It was so film noir. So Veronica Lake. How would I look with my hair combed over one eye? Too bad I'm not a blonde anymore. Or tall. Or svelte. Or beautiful.

Or maybe Lauren Bacall? She was so cool in *To Have and Have Not*, when she turned around and said to Bogey, "...you don't have to say anything and you don't have to do anything.

"Oh, maybe just whistle. You know how to whistle, don't you Steve? You just put your lips together and..."

Chapter Thirty

"...blow me," Joe Attanasio wheezed and rattled, nearly choking in his anger. He was so mad he even forgot to do his Elvis routine. "All right, you lousy broad, we'll be there tomorrow night."

I hung up the phone and looked at John. "That went well, don't you think?" I was shaking like a leaf. "That guy scares the shit out of me."

John took off his headphones and gave me a hug. "You're doing fine. No one is going to get hurt here."

Houston paced the ceiling above us. He stopped just long enough to grumble down, "Yeah, heard that one before. That's what they said at the Titanic. That's what they said at the San Francisco earthquake. That's what they said at Pompei. That's what they said before the bomb went off at the World News Magazine Building."

Just another one of Houston's not-so-subtle attempts to let us know how much he disapproved. I ignored him.

"Let's get the next guy up to bat before I lose my nerve or my momentum. Or both." I dialed Ted Cochran's private office.

"Cochran here," he boomed into the phone.

"You don't have to yell, Mr. Cochran, I can hear you just fine. This is Matilda MacNamara. I'm sure you know who I am."

"Damn right. You're the assassin that slaughtered my ninth-hole green."

Oops. That came out of left field. I gave John the dirtiest look I could muster up and mouthed: You told him?!

John waved me off and mouthed back: Not me.

"Do you have any idea how much it cost to repair the damage? What are you going to do about it? Let's talk money here. Or let's talk jail."

"Funny you should mention that, Ted." I took a deep breath and launched into my script. "This is a shakedown, buster. I've got all the goods."

"Goods? What goods? What are you talking about?"

"If you're smart, you'll shut your trap and listen." I played part of the tape for him just enough for him to hear his own voice and Joe Attanasio. On the other end of the connection his breathing was uneven, but he didn't say anything. So, I finished my lines. "If you and your pals don't cough up a cool 'mil' by tomorrow night, I'm handing these over to the coppers."

"Coppers? Who the hell writes your material?"

I didn't know what to say. That wasn't in the script.

"What if I said: Go ahead, call the 'coppers'?" he snorted.

That wasn't in the script either. "Then..." Come on, Tildy. Think. Think. Think. "...you dirty rat, I'm sending you up the river to Sing-Sing." It was my very best Cagney.

John had this stunned look on his face. "Stop ad-libbing," he whispered fiercely and shook the script at me. "He's bluffing."

Cochran said, "I'm not bluffing."

What is he? Psychic? "Well, me either." We were still off the script. "Ask your old pal Joe about me. He'll tell you I mean business. And I do mean business, Teddy. So, I'll see you tomorrow. It's B.Y.O.C."

"Huh?" he said.

"Bring your own cash." I hung up.

"I can't freakin' believe you two," Houston said scornfully, but I knew he was trying to cover his nerves. "Sing-Sing. Coppers? I should have written this."

"That would have been nice, but you were off somewhere playing hard to get, weren't you?"

"That hurts," Houston pouted. "You know I was only trying to protect you, Tildy."

Can't stay mad at the Disco King for too long. "I know, sweetie, I'm just glad you're on board now." I noticed that John and the two technicians he brought with him were trying to pretend I wasn't talking to thin air.

You're probably thinking if I ignored Houston, I would have looked more like a sane person in the first place. But you try faking normalcy when there's a ghost in your house. See how far you get.

John handed me the last phone number. "One more, Tildy, then we're done."

"For now you mean."

As I dialed Wade Johnson's house, he added, "Try to stick to the script this time."

"Do try, Tildy. Seeing as how it's such a prosaic masterpiece," Houston burst into a fit of giggling.

"Smart ass."

Wade Johnson responded, "Pardon me?"

"Oh, Wade," I added a little lilt to my voice. "It's Tildy."

This one went a lot smoother than it had with Joe or Ted. Wade thought the whole thing was a real hoot. So, when I wrapped it up, with: "I'll see you here tomorrow."

"Wouldn't miss it for the world. I knew there was more to you than meets the eye, you vixen." He laughed again. "Blackmail, huh? Doesn't that beat all? You cute little sack o' shit."

Well, at least he said "cute."

His reaction kinda surprised me. But I guess when you spend your life bull-shitting, womanizing and cheating the taxpayers, very little catches you off guard. You can even manage to take blackmail in stride.

The technicians set the equipment to record any incoming calls and left. Yazzie went out to his car and brought in a small duffel bag. He went over to the sofa and bounced lightly on it — right on top of Houston. "This should be fine."

Houston sighed in ecstasy, "Oh, John."

I was still strung tighter than a piano wire. "Houston, cut it out. John, what are you talking about?"

John laced his fingers behind his head and leaned back against the sofa arm.

I thought Houston would orgasm.

"Geezus," I muttered under my breath.

Houston went on the defense, "Well, it's been a long dry spell."

"I'm not letting you out of my sight until this is over and those men are rotting in my jail. So, if you have an extra pillow, I'll just camp out here."

"Oh," I said, hoping my immense relief wasn't too obvious. "I do have a spare bedroom."

"No, this is better. I can keep watch from here."

Houston was curling around John like an eel. I figured any closer and this deal would really get X-rated. I felt a sense of obligation to save John further embarrassment. "John dear, you're laying in the middle of Houston and he's getting very amorous."

John froze. "He's what? I am?" He started to get up, then he eased back. And I swear I saw a smile on his handsome lips.

Guess he didn't want to be saved after all.

I left the room.

* * * * *

Later that night, John and I ate pizza and popcorn and watched old movies with Houston until the wee hours. We were too keyed up to sleep anyway. In between videos, John told us all about his reconciliation with Big John. Houston and I cried a little bit about it. It was so beautiful. Father and son together again and on the same wave length.

An earlier trip to the local Blockbuster netted the night's entertainment. John the Romantic picked out *Casablanca*. Houston the Professional asked us to bring back *All the Presidents Men*. And Tildy, Detective to the Dead, rented *The Maltese Falcon*, to fine-tune my technique.

At the movie store, John and I noticed the obvious stares of the two older women behind the counter. We made it a point to walk up and down the aisles, holding hands and making goo-goo eyes at each other. We were pretty sure that by morning, if not later that very night, news of our torrid affair would be all over the state.

On the way back to my house, John turned to me and said hesitantly, "You know Tildy, this romance thing could work out pretty good for me. If you don't mind too much, you could be my cover, so to speak."

"Hell no, I don't mind. No heavy dates lined up in my future." Especially after my last one! "And I like you John, I like you a lot."

About two-thirty John crashed on the sofa. Haggis and I headed upstairs to bed, but sleep was an on-again, off-again companion. Can't imagine why. There was nothing to worry about. Chief Bill and Sheriff John and about a thousand cops would be everywhere — inside and out. Nothing was going to happen to me. John had promised Houston. John and Bill had both promised me.

Then why was I so frightened?

I closed my eyes, pulled Haggis' warm little body closer and tried to relax.

* * * * *

A bubble bath. I'm taking a bubble bath. Mounds and mounds of frothy bubbles caress my body. The room is heavy with the scent of Opium. Dozens of flickering candles wash the room in a warm glow. Ahhhh. I lie back, my head on the satin neck pillow from the Sharper Image catalogue. It is heaven. Placid, quiet, soothing.

A melody plays — softly at first, then louder. Wait a minute. That's Jailhouse Rock. Jailhouse Rock? *Elvis?*

"Everybody in the whole cell block was dancin' to the Jailhouse Rock."

Aw, no. Not Elvis. If it's Elvis — it must be...

I hear it now. That wet, sucking Darth Vader sound. Oh, shit. Joe. It's him. I knew I shouldn't have had that third piece of pizza.

He's outside the bathroom window, riding his electric wheelchair through the air. The bastard. Behind him a dark funnel cloud snakes toward the house, catching Joe, holding him aloft to circle and circle. He laughs, then chokes and coughs up a wad of phlegm. Now it's a cackle and he snatches Haggis from the cyclone.

Haggis struggles and cries: Mom, help.

Oh, Haggis, I'm coming. But I can't get out of the tub. I try and I try. But I can't get out.

The wheelchair morphs into a broom. Joe turns into the Wicked Witch of the West, and jets across the boiling sky to write in blood red letters: S U R R E N D E R T I L D Y. He turns and comes straight at the window growing larger and larger until the glass SHATTERS!

I scream as blood and water are everywhere, pounding me again and again. I try to rise from the tub, to run. But I can't. The crimson water comes crashing down on me, holding me under. Haggis, where are you?

I can't breathe. And suddenly I'm drowning in a sea of...

Chapter Thirty-One

"...Miracle Herb Clay, you say?" The red, gritty, flax-seed crap squished between my toes, under my arms, and a couple of other places that were really uncomfortable.

"Mmmm," Grace grunted.

I looked over at her face, covered in the same green goop I was wearing. Her eyes were closed, her jaw clenched.

No other explanation, her looking so miserable, except, "You got this gushy stuff up your crack too?"

She rolled her head to the side and, without opening her eyes, said dryly, "I told you to wear the briefs. But would you listen? No."

To get my mind off the crud oozing into my pores, I thought of Officer Barnett waiting none too patiently outside. He'd made it pretty clear this was pain-in-the-butt babysitting duty, watching the crazy lady and all, and if he was Chief of Police, I'd be the one behind bars or in a straight jacket. Although, he perked up when I mentioned he could spend the day watching all those rich, firm bodies in for a tune-up.

Grace, God bless her soul, had made appointments for us to spend the day at the spa. And, man, when they say Paradise Spa, they ain't kidding. It's a little piece of Heaven nestled beneath Kachina Woman Rock.

A cluster of red stucco casitas and haciendas sat tucked among the jade juniper bushes. Turquoise pools sparkled in the sun. It was the idyllic respite for the rich, the beautiful, the famous, and the desperate, i.e., Tildy MacNamara.

As totally relaxing as it was, soaking in the red shit, followed by a full-body warm stone massage, I just couldn't keep my mind off things. Plus, I had to keep an eye out for Ted Cochran. After all, he did own the place. And wouldn't it be a major fubar if I ran into him?

"If something goes wrong tonight, Grace, will you take Haggis?"

"Sure. Why not?" It was brisk and to the point.

I opened my eyes and looked at her. She was on her stomach, her head half-buried in the table's headrest, the towel laying across her keister. I couldn't see her face. "Something wrong?"

She didn't answer.

"If it's a problem, Chloe would take him." Had I upset her? She was probably just worried about me. "I mean, it's semantics, right? Nothing's going to happen. I'm protected by the best lawmen in the state."

"This ghost, this Houston Powers guy..." she began.

"Yesssss?" My voice quivered as the masseuse gave my back a final pounding.

"You talk to him?"

"Yeah, English and everything."

"Well, doesn't he know who killed him?"

"Duh, Grace," I moaned as warm, flat stones turned my muscles to butter. "That's what this is all about. If he knew who murdered him, he would have gone into the light like he was supposed to, and I wouldn't be throwing a party for the mob."

"What about that other stuff?" Now it was her turn to sound like a Munchkin as the tiny but really, really strong Chinese lady laid into her.

"What other stuff?"

"All that murder stuff with Bolles. And the land scam. What does that have to do with the reporter being killed?"

"It's all tied together. That's why he was in Sedona, to expose the land scam and find out more about the Bolles murder."

"And that other stuff you showed me? What was it? Freedom fighters?"

"Ancient history. Happened a long time before he was killed. It didn't have anything to do with him being here."

We stepped into the warm, soft robes the two attendants held for us, and shuffled our slippered feet down the hall to the meditation room.

The sun poured in through the skylights, heating the room to sleep-inducing warmth. Its rays penetrated the crystals, casting a shifting rainbow of light throughout the room.

My lids grew heavy.

Grace must have been feeling it, too. She was quiet for a long time. The solemn beauty of the Crystal Room inspired meditation and introspection, and naps.

"I wish you didn't have to do this, Tildy," she said drowsily. "Maybe you should call it off."

"I can't. I have to do it. I don't feel as if I have a choice." I yawned. "Don't laugh, Grace, but I think it's my destiny."

She opened one eye and squinted at me. "Give me a break, Obi Wan. Next thing you'll be telling me you've been seduced by the dark side."

"Well, you never know," I mused, half-asleep, "could be fun."

We slept for a half-hour before they came and got us for our beauty appointments.

Facials, waxing, manicures, pedicures, haircut, styling, makeup. The whole schmeer. And thank God for that. A girl should look her very best for blackmail.

* * * * *

It was seven forty-five that night. Fifteen minutes and counting to liftoff. The house seemed so empty without the patter of little feet. I'd taken Haggis to Chloe for safekeeping.

Although there *was* the patter of *big* feet here and there: two deputies upstairs, Sheriff John crouching among the Saran wrap and bags of Chips Ahoy in the pantry.

Then you got Chief Parrish and half his force hiding outside.

Yup — empty, all right.

The phone rang and I went to pick it up, feeling like a TV heroine. Brave. In control. Lethal. Buffy the Gangster Slayer at your service.

I answered the phone, trying to keep my voice normal. "Hello?"

"Matilda? It's me." Andrew's voice sucked me right back to Chicago, back to the immaculate condo with no trace of me in it anywhere, back to the incompetent, helpless little woman I used to be.

I didn't say anything, not trusting my voice or the powerful emotions surging up inside me, fighting to get out, to unload themselves on his rounded but capable shoulders — that same old trap. Why did this happen every time I heard his voice? And when would it stop?

"You okay, honey?" he asked, "Something wrong?"

Deep breath. "I..." And another one. "Andrew, I..." It didn't work. I choked.

"Are you crying? Are you hurt?" His voice rose.

"I don't know if I can do it, Andrew. I just don't..."

"Come home, Matilda." He always had an answer. "Come back here where you belong. I'll take care of you. Just like before."

But hardly ever the right answer. Just like before? Well, there's a sobering thought. And here's another one. This is where it would stop.

And now the intrepid Tildy reaches into her bag, and pulls out — ta-da! — Mister Pointy, her trusty weapon. She's ready to take on the world. Ready to meet the gangsters. Ready to drive Mister Pointy (no phallic reference intended) straight into the frozen heart of her ex-husband. I was back from the realm of the chicken-hearted. "I have to go now, Andrew."

"No. We should talk about whatever is bothering you, Matilda."

"I don't need to talk to you. Not about this, not about anything. Not any more." It felt so good to say those words.

"Don't be stupid, Matilda." Stupid? Did he really say "stupid?" Just when you start to like the guy — he screws up again. "Let me be here for you. Lean on me." And thank the stars for small favors.

I didn't want to lean on him. And as a familiar voice echoed in my mind, I couldn't help myself. "And with my vote, Andrew, you are the weakest link." Snicker, snicker. "Good bye." I hung up, took a deep breath.

Upstairs I could hear the deputies laughing their butts off.

John's bass voice rumbled from the kitchen, "Atta girl."

Houston applauded from the stairs.

That's when the doorbell rang.

That's when my heart stopped.

Feet, don't fail me now. But I was glued to the floor.

The doorbell chimed again. *Ding Dong.*

The witch is dead. Which old witch?...

Chapter Thirty-Two

"...you stinkin' bitch!" From the front porch, Attanasio bellowed as loud as his wheezy voice would allow.

"Tildy? You home?" That was Wade.

Showtime. But my feet still didn't seem to know it.

"Open the door," Sheriff John's hoarse whisper found my ears.

I jerked into motion, pried my feet from the floor, took a deep breath and...

"Good evening, gentlemen."

There they were. Wade, looking dapper as usual, in a coffee-colored three-piece Western-style suit. He was holding a beige felt Stetson in one hand and a bouquet of daisies in the other. He was smiling.

Ted Cochran, on the other hand, was glaring at me. He was red-faced, breathing hard, with his hands balled into fists. The hair plugs hadn't quite taken yet and he looked like a half-plucked kid's doll, weird little tufts sticking out everywhere. His belly was barely contained in a navy blue Ralph Lauren golf shirt. The khaki slacks should have been a size or two bigger. You couldn't see his waist for the dunlap — you know, his belly done lapped over?

Then there was Joe. Black Elvis wig, white leather jumpsuit, short white cape and white patent-leather boots with the toes cut out so the atrociously long nails could curl out and over.

"Get a load of these dorks," Houston commented. "God help us."

"These here are for you, little gal." Wade thrust the daisies at me and stepped inside.

I gulped. Was that some kind of message that I might be pushing up daisies soon?

Ted grunted and followed Wade inside.

Joe rolled in at full speed, and if I hadn't jumped back, he would have lopped off a couple of my toes. He was in a different wheelchair than that first night. This one had a skull and crossbones on the shiny black back-piece with licks of red and orange flame. Probably his choice for showdowns and weddings.

Always gracious, I motioned the "gentlemen" into the parlor, then went about my hostess duties.

"Hors d'oeuvre?" I offered a tray containing shredded beef empañadas, chile con queso, chipotle salsa, blue corn tortilla chips, and a couple of peanut butter and banana sandwiches for the King. The thoughtful party giver always takes every guest's needs into consideration, no matter how friggin' bizarre they are.

"What are you, nuts? You feeding these guys? You're the target. They ought to be offering *you* the last meal." When I gasped, Houston hurriedly added, "Sorry, forget I said that."

I returned with a second tray of cocktails. The chartreuse I handed to Wade.

He smiled, winked and toasted me, "You're one of a kind, missy."

Joe had his mouth full of peanut butter and bananas. "Got milk?"

Ted, obviously lacking the finer points of etiquette, jammed a couple of empañadas in his mouth and growled, "Let's quit dicking around and get down to it."

I went over and took three envelopes from the secretary drawer, handing one to each man.

Wade took it from me and leaned over to whisper in my ear. "You look lovely tonight, Tildy."

Above us, Houston stuck his finger down his throat. "Gag me."

"Thank you, Wade," I smiled, trying to hide my nerves. "I gave a lot of thought as to what I'd wear tonight."

And it was true. I had. Upstairs, my bed was buried beneath at least a dozen outfits I'd tried and rejected before finally settling on a pair of black rayon slacks, and a red top under a long black vest with brush strokes of spicy cayenne and white. You ever try to find something that's both attractive yet roomy enough to cover a flak jacket? Carnelian hearts with silver doodads were at my ears and throat. I looked good if I say so myself. Of course, the whole effect was pretty much spoiled by my white Nikes. But when you're scamming the mob, a good pair of running shoes just might come in handy. Haute couture be damned.

"You have what you came after, boys. I believe it's customary to pay on delivery."

Joe reached under his cape and pulled out a big old six-shooter. Houston and I both jumped back. Hello.

"Now hold on there, Joseph." Wade politicked. "We made a deal with this little gal." He tossed back the Chartreuse. "I've done some sorry things in my life; cheating the Navajos was one of the sorriest. I draw the line at murder." Good old Wade.

"Go ahead. Kill her, Joe. Shoot her." Ted, the blood-thirsty son of a gun, wanted his revenge served straight off the grill.

"You covered?" The King cocked his pistol and drawled.

"Covered?" I gulped.

"The gentleman means do you have a contingency plan if this doesn't work out." Houston explained from behind me.

"Oh, covered. Of course I'm covered. You didn't think I'd be stupid enough to not have insurance? Anything happens to me, the tapes go to Sheriff Yazzie." It was hard to stay in the game when all I wanted to do was tear off the damn hundred-pound flak jacket before what little cleavage I had was flattened beyond repair.

"Oh, Christ, no. Not Sheriff Yazzie?" Joe chortled. "I'm shaking in my boots."

"The ones without the toes?" Houston chirped. "Will someone please get this man some nail clippers?"

Ted joined in. "You don't mean the same Sheriff whose daddy's balls we got in our pocket?"

"Honey," Wade slid in, smooth as glass, "you didn't think *we'd* be stupid enough to not have insurance."

"Does this mean you're not going to...?"

"Pay you?" It was a chorus. All three buttheads chimed in at the same time. All that was missing was a little harmony and the doo-ah-dittys.

Joe whipped around and headed for the door. "The King is outta here."

As Elvis would say: *It's now or never.* "Not so fast, bozo." Was that my voice cracking?

"Get 'em, Tildy," Houston urged me on.

Joe came to a screeching halt, then whipped back around to face me. "Bozo? Hell, I'll just kill you now and be done with it." His hand shook as he tried to lift the heavy gun.

"Like you killed Don Bolles?" There it was, out there in the open for God and everybody to hear.

Nobody said anything for a second, then Joe piped in, "Watch what you're saying, baby. You know you got no proof to back that up."

When you're right, you're right. "Maybe I don't have any proof you had Bolles blown all to hell. But how about Houston Powers? Maybe I have proof you killed him."

I was screwed. It was in their eyes, and I knew even before they said in unison, "Who?"

"Houston Powers? World-famous Pulitzer Prize reporter? Houston Powers? The reporter who nailed Sasha the Terrorist, and who came up here to nail your sorry butts for the seventies land scam after the Bolles' murder? Houston Powers who you had mercilessly run down in the road like a dog?" Dear God, please let one of them look alarmed or afraid or even awake.

"Dog? What do you mean 'dog'?"

"Knock it off, Houston," I hissed under my breath.

Wade spoke slowly, "I don't know who this man was, Tildy. I never even heard of him, much less have anything to do with killing him."

"What the hell are you talking about? Yeah, we fucked them Indians. And, yeah, we scammed the Feds. Why would we murder someone we never knew?" Cochran was such a sweetheart. "Stupid bitch. Just kill her now, Joe."

My last chance of saving Houston was wearing a white leather jump suit and staring through blue-lensed aviator glasses. He smiled, whirled around and headed for the door. Ted and Wade followed. Wade turned back at the door and made a phone of his thumb and pinky indicating he'd be calling.

In your dreams, asshole.

I turned away tiredly. There would be no confession tonight. We were screwed.

A big sigh from behind me and I could tell Houston knew it too. "Time to show 'em or fold 'em, Tildy."

I nodded and said loud enough to be heard in the kitchen, "You're not going anywhere, you scumbags. You're busted."

John stormed in, gun in hand, "Police. Freeze."

"What a man!" Houston sighed.

Joe spun around. "Bitch!" and the gun went off, taking out my Tiffany lamp.

I hit the floor and covered my head, muttering, "Aw, my mother sent me that lamp from New York when she went to see *The Producers*."

Cops swarmed in like killer bees and manhandled the three cursing felons into submission.

Just like in the movies, the bad guys were hauled off in due course. And things got real quiet, real fast.

John hung around a minute to say, "You were awesome, sweetie," then more sadly, "Tell Houston I'm..."

"Tell him it's okay," Houston said.

"He knows, John. We both know," I said. "John, if they didn't kill him, who did?"

"Beats me," he said. "We'll just have to figure out something else."

But we were all aware there was no "something else." Maybe he wasn't murdered after all. Maybe it was just a hit-and-run.

I felt awful. It hadn't worked out at all. And here the poor guy was, all chances of a normal afterlife gone forever.

"I'm so sorry, honey," I said to him.

"Oh, that's okay," he said sweetly. "You tried. That's all anybody can do."

Wait a minute. That's okay? "What's going on, Houston? You're never this subdued."

"Nothing. Why?"

Way too nonchalant. My voice lowered threateningly "Houston."

"Well, it's just that I sort of remember now that maybe I never really got going on my investigation here. Maybe I kinda spent all my time with John. And maybe these guys aren't the ones who murdered me because they never even knew I was a threat to them. Because I never got around to asking them any questions or checking up on them."

I couldn't believe what I was hearing. "What? Now you remember?" I was completely blown away. "If they didn't know who you were, why would they want you dead? Right now I'm ready to kill you myself — but what would *their* motive be?"

I could tell he was as shaken up as I was. "Motive?"

"Mmm. You've heard of that word. Right? I mean, I'm a complete novice and even I know murder requires a motive."

"Uhhhhh...."

And that really pissed me off. "I can't freakin' believe you sent me after them. God dammit, those guys could have killed me. In fact, they almost did. Now you tell me they didn't even know who you were?! What in the hell is wrong with you anyway?"

He came right back at me. "I'll tell you what's wrong with me. I spent the last twenty-five years cooling my heels on that front porch out there," he jabbed his finger at the door, "waiting for someone to set me free. Twenty-five years, Tildy. And when that somebody finally does come along. Look what I get — a chocolate-addicted, whiney-assed, Chicago society matron. Yeah, you worked your butt off. I'll give you that. But it was me who told you what to do and how to do it. Every single thing. You didn't know shit."

"Matron! You calling me a matron! That's so low, Houston. Gay men can be so bitchy."

"Aaaah," he shrieked as smoke rose from his shoulders. "I'm outta here."

"What are you yelling at me for? This is your fault. It's all your fault."

Houston disappeared in a cloud.

"Chickenshit," I screamed. "Stay here and fight like a man."

But the room was empty. Really empty. I was completely alone and it was the first time in a long time. I headed to the kitchen for a chocolate fix. Seeing as how I was an addict and all. But all I could find was a half-empty bottle of Yoo-Hoo. Any port in a storm. I grabbed it and went back into the living room.

My mind skittered over the craziness of the last few weeks. Everything I had gone through. All the risks I had taken. All for nothing. I felt incredibly sorry for myself. And the tears came. I sat on the sofa and boo-hooed for a good fifteen minutes.

Then it occurred to me it might not be so bad having Houston around forever. I mean, there are worse things in life than being kept company by a funny, intelligent, sophisticated man.

And it hadn't been for nothing. Look what I did. If it wasn't for me, there would be no justice for the Navajo tribe. And if it wasn't for me, Big John and Little John wouldn't have reconciled. I helped give Minnie closure over the death of her son. And whether it was a good thing or not (the final vote was yet to be cast), I played a vital role in an ex-wife's revenge on a peccadillo husband. Not to mention how far I'd come in the process.

I'd been looking at it all wrong. My Yoo-Hoo wasn't half empty. It was half full of...

Chapter Thirty-Three

"...horse manure. You were just jogging by and found the bomb? That's not even a good lie." Chief Parrish pushed Donnie down. "Sit your ass in that chair. You as much as breathe wrong," he shoved his gun into Donnie's ear, "Tildy's gonna have to repaint her kitchen."

Holy shit. Donnie was in my kitchen. I was glued against the counter. My breath came in ragged spurts. I was shaking all over like a vibrating bed in a cheap motel.

"You okay?" Bill asked, his words full of concern. It obviously never occurred to him how this would affect me.

"No." I couldn't take my eyes off Donnie. Handcuffed and beat up, he was still my worst nightmare even if right then he looked more scared than I was.

I kept staring at his left ear. It didn't look quite right to me, like maybe a piece of it was gone. It was bloody as hell. Had he been sparring with Mike Tyson?

And there was this nasty, oozing gouge on his neck.

His hair looked like he'd had a go-around with a Vegematic and lost. Huge clumps were missing.

"I think it's a gorilla, " Bill said wryly. "You think it's a gorilla?"

"Oh, yeah." And in my kitchen, yet!

"But is it your gorilla?"

"I'm not laying claim to him but he is the one who tried to kill me." I was beginning to relax a little. It didn't look like Donnie would be making any quick moves with the barrel of Bill's gun stuck in his ear. "How'd you get him?"

"This big old monkey was outside planting a bomb. Looked like he was planning on blowing you and this house to kingdom come."

"A bomb!?" How could that word be so casually applied to me and my home? "Tell me you didn't say bomb?"

"Damnedest thing. He got the drop on me and we went at it. The sucker was kicking my ass, too. About near beat my brains out."

I noticed then Bill's uniform was ripped and covered in mud, and his face was bruised and scraped.

"Then it happened," he said with wonder in his voice. "I heard it before I saw it. A metal sound. Clacking. And then all of a sudden this big old monkey jumps off me and I look up and see it." His face was sheepish. "Now don't laugh. It was a pair of gardening shears — just hanging there. Chopping the bejeezus out of old Donnie here. He was screaming like a girl."

I was scared and nervous, but I couldn't help myself. I had to laugh. "Yeah, he tends to do that sometimes."

The air conditioner kicked on with a loud clank. Donnie gave a little cry of fright and lunged up. He would have bolted if Bill hadn't jammed the gun right up against his throat.

"I'll shoot your hairy ass, gorilla, if you don't put it back in that chair."

Donnie's eyes rolled wildly. Spittle flew as he whined, "Don't let it get me, sir. Please. Please. Don't let it get me. Take me to jail. I'll be safe there. This place is the doorway to Hell. Get me out of here."

Bill smiled, a really big, smug smile. "Something you want to tell us then, Donnie?"

"It was the boss. Him and his friends thought after they got the tapes, I should blow up the house and this crazy bitch with it. And before that — the bathtub, Canyon de Chelly — that was me, too. Just doing whatever they said. I'll make a statement. Testify in court. Say it on *Sixty Minutes*. Whatever you want. Anything," he was crying. "Just get me outta here!"

Bill patted him on his clumpy head. "Hold that thought, son. We'll be outta here soon enough." He laughed. "In the meantime I'll protect you from her. You hear, Tildy? You stop that voodoo stuff now." He winked broadly.

Enough with the fooling around. Donnie, scared or not, hurt or not, was dangerous. "Just keep your gun on him, Bill. And lock him up for the rest of the millennium."

With his free hand he scratched his chin. "I have to say I've never seen shears act that way before. Is there really something to this psychic stuff? Was that you saving my life, Tildy?"

"No. Not me, but I may know who it was."

Three officers came barreling in and, after making sure the Chief was okay, they took charge of Donnie.

Bill thanked me again for saving his life. Rather than trying to explain, I just said, "Anytime."

On his way out he mentioned how he'd like to get together sometime. Said he'd give me a call. I was way too tired to deal with it. So I just smiled. Suddenly I was the belle of the ball and my dance card was full. Who'd o' thunk it?

I shut the door behind him, locked it and leaned against it a minute, the events of the night replaying in my head.

Now you know and I know it wasn't me that went after Donnie with the garden shears. It was my resident ghost, lovable old Houston. Even when he was pissed off at me, he was still my knight in shining bellbottoms.

I walked all around the house calling him, but it was pretty obvious he wasn't there. I remembered when he "manifested" before and wondered if it was the same thing, if he was laid up somewhere trying to recuperate. Let's face it, he ain't exactly the Energizer Bunny. It worried me. It was so bad the last time. Could he do it over and over and still come back? Would he even want to after that terrible fight we had?

I couldn't wait to congratulate him on getting the best of Donnie and on things in general.

Maybe we didn't get the jerks for murdering Houston, but we'd get them on defrauding the government with their land scam and, since Donnie was singing like a canary, we would also get them on conspiracy to commit murder. All in all, we'd done okay. With the bad guys in jail, and Houston off doing his rejuvenation, maybe I'd finally get a decent night's sleep. And God knows I needed it.

The house was dead quiet and empty. After all the commotion, the letdown was brutal. I was bone tired, felt like I just fell off the hearse and they forgot to come back and get me. All I wanted to do was crawl into bed, pull the covers over my head and hide.

That wasn't in the cards.

The phone rang. I looked at my watch. What now? Geezus, it was eleven-forty.

"Hello?"

It was John calling to make sure I was okay and to see if I wanted an officer to keep watch.

"Thanks, but no thanks," I said. "You got them all, big guy. You da man."

"I hate it when people say that." He hung up.

The phone rang again. "What'd you forget?"

A metallic voice raised the hair on the back of my neck. "You the one nosing around about that reporter's murder?"

"Is this a trick question?"

"I got something that'll blow your investigation wide open. Think you can get your hands on some cash? Five grand?"

My mind raced. The store receipts. I still hadn't made the bank drop from all of Simon's sales as well as the day before. All totaled, I had at least five grand. "Maybe. Why?"

"I know who did it. The killer's dead now, too. But that shouldn't make no nevermind to you. You just want to solve the case. Right? Bring the money and meet me at Slide Rock at midnight, I'll tell you who did it. And I've got proof." The voice paused, then, "I see any pigs, I'm outta there." The line went dead.

I sank down on the couch, the phone still clutched in my hand. Figured this would happen when Houston was incommunicado.

I debated. To go or not to go. That is the question whether 'tis nobler in the mind to suffer the slings and arrows of the pesky friggin' ghost or to take arms against my bad case of the jitters, and by opposing, end them.

I closed my eyes and tried to make it come. My psychic power, that is. Tried to force some kind of message or vision to my poor brain. Nothing happened. Not even a glimmer. Why do I even bother? Let's face it. This thing owns me. I don't even begin to own it. Most things I find out the hard way. And when I do get something, it usually winds up making me look like a fool.

A wise man once said, "If the spirits wanted you to know what's out there at Slide Rock, they'd have told you."

Slide Rock. The very words made me shiver.

Slide Rock. Slowly I turned... step-by-step. Inch-by-inch...

Chapter Thirty-Four

...digit-by-digit. My trembling fingers punched out John's number. But on the other end of the line, his voice mail picked up. Maybe he was still booking those guys over at the jail, or on his way to Flag to the county lock-up. I tried the main number, and asked the dispatcher to put me through to him.

After a minute or two, she came back with, "Sorry. Can't reach him. Want to leave a message?"

Damn right. So I did, then turned right around and called Bill.

Same bloody thing — out of touch. They'd page him and have him get "right back to me."

Where's a cop when you really need one?

Next? Grace. Crap — no answer.

Joaquin? Dammit!

Where was everybody? Someone throw a party and leave my name off the invite list? Or what?

I mulled it over.

All the bad guys were already in jail, so they shouldn't be a problem.

And according to my late-night caller, Houston's murderer was dead, so he shouldn't be a problem, unless of course he's lying and he *is* the murderer — then I have a big problem.

I had an S.O.S. in to both the Sheriff and the Chief of Police. Surely by the time I got out to the creek, I'd have backup.

Sure, I know what you're thinking. Not the safe bet. Right? Well, all I can say in my defense is that my recent successes must have gone straight to my head. I stupidly believed I could handle anything that came along at Slide Rock.

Slide Rock. There was nothing to be afraid of, unless you count the completely scary stuff that happened out there before. The night chase. The Edgar Allen Poe premature-burial scenario. A dance with the Grim Reaper. But *that* happened to Houston. Not me.

It felt like I was really on the verge of getting the answer, and losing that pesky Disco Duck, sending him along to that big dance floor in the sky.

If that sounds harsh, consider the circumstances. I was operating in my tough-cookie mode. You've gotta be tough to pick up your keys, go out to your car, drive down the road knowing you're about to come to face-to-face with the most haunting nightmare of your life.

And that's what I had to do. I have no earthly idea how I did it. Or even why I did it. But I did it.

* * * * *

Slide Rock Park was totally deserted. No sign of anyone, anywhere. Not even a night guard. The single security light by the entry gate was shattered. Uh-oh. What better reason to call in the cavalry?

I got on my cell and gave everyone in the galaxy another try. But the signal kept cutting in and out and I never got through.

The latch on the gate was broken, so I could drive right in. Another bad sign. I knew the State of Arizona was johnny-on-the-spot with repairs, so it was a sure bet this just happened — probably for my benefit. Made me a little nervous — okay, fine. I was shaking like a leaf.

I prayed John or Bill was already on the way, prayed I wasn't really out in the wilderness on my own at the mercy of some criminal mastermind.

I eased the car through the entrance, then along the foot path all the way past the settlers' house as far as the old apple-packing shed.

There I was. Just me and my shadow.

And my Louisville Slugger — good for head-thumping.

And my Mace spray — good for really messing up bad guys.

And my Swiss Army knife — good for opening wine bottles or whatever.

And my Mag-Lite — totally excellent for bashing in general.

And my cell phone — which was, well, good for pretty much nothing out there.

Yeah, I was loaded for bear, baby.

I got out and locked the car, keyed the alarm, hefted the bat over my shoulder and set out for Slide Rock, muttering to myself, "Houston, you better be eternally friggin' grateful for this."

I jumped at every rustle, every hoot, every whisper — even at some things that probably didn't even make noise — waving the flashlight spastically this way and that way. No way anybody was going to sneak up on me.

I was beginning to hate this freakin' place. The shadows of the apple trees, cool and inviting during the day, became sinister and threatening in the moonlight. A crazy person could be lurking in there, biding their time, waiting for just the right moment to strike. Or maybe the crazy one was walking down to the creek with her makeshift arsenal.

But no one jumped me. I made it just fine. All the way down to the big flat rock over the water, where I paced nervously and waited.

And waited.

And waited.

After a while, I began to think it was really nice there — quiet except for the soft sound of rushing water and the occasional hoot of an owl. A few lazy clouds played hide and seek with the moon. A soft breeze cooled the air to perfection.

I shined the flashlight on my watch. Twelve-twenty. Where was he? This mystery man — did I miss him somehow? Was he...?

Whack! Breaking glass tinkled. "Holy shit!" I jumped as the piercing wail of my car alarm shattered the stillness. "My car. My beautiful car. The money!"

I ran, slowly at first, then faster and faster as anger overcame fear.

"Bastard!" I gritted.

My car was in the exact spot I left it, screaming its head off. I shut the damn thing off and noticed right away that the windshield and driver's side windows were both smashed. I opened the door and, sure enough, no bank bag. I whipped around, shining my light everywhere.

But the jerk was long gone, taking the money, leaving me with the shaft. "This really pisses me off!" I shouted at him, hoping he was still within hearing distance. "Get back here. Pay me what you owe me, dammit!"

What was I? Nuts? What was I going to do if he did hear me? Better yet, what was I going to do if he came back?

I tried Bill on my cell phone again. But there was no signal.

The moon slid behind a cloud. A chill wind lifted my hair. In the distance a cougar screamed. My blood went cold as a voice came to life inside my head: *What the hell do you think you're doing? Get in the car and boogie!*

Okay. I got in and turned it over.

Hurry, the voice said. *Trouble's coming. Find someplace safe.*

I never argue with the voice when I'm out in the middle of no-man's land in the dead of the night and my car's been trashed. It's not the smart move.

I looked down and saw that my GPS unit was busted. My guess was, it would be completely useless. "What else?" I was afraid to get out and check the car over. I didn't know who or what was out there.

"I'll just drive real slow and easy." Not a problem, that was the only way I could drive since I could barely see out the shattered windshield.

The voice wasn't having any of that. *Move it. Move it. Get out of here. Get away!*

"Okay, Voice. Just hold your horses." I pulled out onto Highway 89-A. "Well damn, Houston. Looks like I let you down again."

I pushed harder on the accelerator and the car went faster. A plan formed in my brain. I'd drive straight to the police station. I'd be safe there. Bill would help me, or maybe Officer Barnett (after all, I *was* his favorite).

But at the first bend in the road, Ms. Genius Detective-to-the-Dead realized her brake line had been cut. I probably should have checked for that, you know, since it happened in the dream and all. But, just like in the dream...

I was so friggin' scared I couldn't think straight.

My car gathered speed, fishtailing at nearly every bend. The headlights careened wildly over the twisting roadway.

The tires squealed as I fought to keep the car on the road. A flash in the rearview mirror nearly blinded me. Lights. Headlights. A car, coming fast, coming too fast.

"What's wrong with those morons?" I muttered under my breath as they bore down on me. "Can't they see I'm in trouble here?"

The old pickup whipped around me, then cut me off. I yanked hard on the wheel and swerved right, momentarily forgetting about the brakes.

I think it was at that point, with my car heading straight for the huge trunk of a big old cottonwood tree, and my foot stomping futilely on the brake pedal, I realized that what was happening to me had happened before.

I'd been set up. Just like Houston.

And I was being stalked. Just like Houston.

But that's where it would stop. The bastard wasn't going to kill me, *not* like Houston.

A split second before my beautiful new Land Cruiser slammed into the tree, I threw it in reverse. The transmission screamed bloody murder and the car stopped dead just inches away from the tree.

"Okay." I popped the seat belt and hit the pavement, looking back over my shoulder every couple of seconds, paranoid as hell but madder than I think I've ever been in my entire life. "I know you're out there," I yelled. "Come and get me."

The voice said, *Are you crazy? Just run. Dammit!*

The pickup came from out of nowhere, screaming around the curve for another go at me. I turned for a look. Big mistake. It was mesmerizing. Hypnotic.

I was a deer caught in the headlights. My heart was a jack hammer pounding in my throat.

I tried to run, but my legs wouldn't cooperate.

The lights were everywhere, blinding me. When I finally got going, my feet sprouted wings. I flew off the pavement, racing for the line of trees along the road. There was safety there. It couldn't follow me into the trees. The truck was almost on top of me when my ankle turned and I went down.

Oh, God help me.

The metal monster roared straight at me. It was huge. It was all I could see. There was no escape. I rolled to the side. But —

Wham!

I cried out. Pain, such horrible pain. I couldn't stand it and thanked God as the waves of blackness began to wash over me until finally there was nothing. Light, then dark, then darker, until —

No light. No sound. Nothing, then I heard...

Chapter Thirty-Five

"...*Seasons don't fear the reaper. Nor do the wind or the sun or the rain. We can be like they are.*"

I came awake slowly. The first thing I felt was the agony in my leg. I tried to turn my head and was rewarded with a sharp stab of pain. Darkness folded around me again and the radio faded.

"...*Come on, baby. Don't fear the reaper.*"

Cool air blew across my face. I was laying on something hard. I tried to rise, to see where I was, but it was pure torture. I fought the blackness threatening to take me again.

The voice: *Stay awake, girl. Stay conscious.*

Me: *What happened? Where am I?*

The voice again: *You got hit by a truck, Miss Genius Ace Detective. You're in the orchard by the house. That's a fresh grave over there, with your name on it.*

Me: *Grave?*

Damn that Simon. He was totally right. Next time I'll pay more attention. I tried to roll over, but there was no way.

Me: *My leg is killing me.*

The voice: *Right. They tend to hurt when they're broken.*

Me: *And my head. Worse than a Chartreuse hangover.*

The voice: *Get your whiny butt up, Tildy. Get help. You could die out here. Just like me.*

Me: *Houston? That you?*

Voice: *Who the hell else would it be? Get up, Tildy. She's going to kill you.*

I sensed somebody was there with me. Who? Beneath the sound of the truck's radio, I became aware of the rhythmic scrape of a shovel against earth. That stopped, to be replaced by the sounds of someone moving around, then coming my way.

Me: *Who is it? Who tried to kill me?*

Houston: *Quiet. Here she comes. Don't move. Play dead. You'll figure it out soon enough. Shhh.*

I was flat on my back in the bed of the pickup. The radio still played Blue Oyster Cult. I thought the reaper thing was a bad sign.

Houston was right. Someone was coming. The muffled footsteps grew closer.

I eased the Mace out of my pocket, flipped it around so it would spray, then hid it inside my closed fist. And waited.

The gate dropped down with a loud clank and a pair of strong hands closed on me.

Houston: *Here it comes. Don't even breathe.*

My leg erupted in complete and total agony as my assailant pulled on my shoulders. From somewhere inside came the strength to stay absolutely still through it all. But the pain in my leg was nothing compared to the barrage of violence that assaulted me psychically.

Image after image crashed into my mind. Horrible scenes of destruction and violence.

Dirty long-haired youths pummel a bank guard bloody while terrified tellers stuff cash into a duffel bag.

An older woman is dragged screaming from the back of a limo and jammed brutally into the trunk of a car.

Two policemen bail out of a burning squad car a second before it explodes in a massive fireball.

A tremendous roar shakes The World News Magazine Building. Smoke and flames boil out into the night. Shards of glass rain down everywhere.

Inside — the fire roars around us. Hot so hot. We run. Houston. Me. And Grace?

The blast chases after us. An exit beckons beyond the wall of fire, but we can't get to it. There are others here trapped and dying. Their screams echo in my head. Young men Freedom Fighters, young women Freedom Fighters, three security guards — one an older widower whose wife died years before — one younger whose woman and young children wait for him at home — the last already dead. The heat and smoke overpower them all. The blaze devours them. Their screams cut us to our very souls.

And the conflagration rises and we are on fire — burning, burning. Houston. Me. And someone who is Grace, but not Grace. Sasha.

Oh, Christ. Grace is Sasha the Terrorist. She's the one who killed Houston. She's the one who ran me down. And she's the one who is dragging me from the truck to my grave.

Auto-pilot is a pretty awesome mechanism when it kicks in. When Grace leaned down to get a better hold on me, without even so much as a thought, I let her have it — a full blast of Mace — right in the kisser.

She let go with a shriek of pain and reeled back. Her cries cut into the night as she fell to her knees and clawed at her face.

Houston: *Run, baby. Get away. Got to get away.*

Grunting with the pain, I rolled over and slid my legs off the edge. I stretched to reach a shovel lying toward the back of the pick-up bed, grabbed it and jammed it down beside my bad leg to use as a crutch.

I hopped — the jarring was excruciating. Every movement made it worse. Terror, adrenaline and rage kept me moving. That and Houston's urgent voice whispering in my mind: *Hurry, Tildy. Hurry. Please don't let her get you.*

I hobbled into the orchard, using the trees for cover. As I moved awkwardly along, more images assailed me, filling my mind, making it hard to see through them.

I saw Sasha's post-conviction escape from a work detail, her frantic cross-country flight. I saw a half-dozen painful cosmetic surgeries that altered her appearance, the donning of a new identity and finally peace among the red rocks of Sedona. Peace, life, happiness, until the man who had orchestrated her capture showed up. And then her life was shattered.

She had to kill Houston. In her panic and desperation, there was no other choice. I knew she would die before going back to jail. And I knew she would kill me when she found me — if I didn't escape or stop her.

Sweat burned my eyes. My ragged breaths came in sobs as I made my way deeper and deeper into the orchard, sensing her pursuit. And my friend confirmed it.

Houston: *Go faster. She's close now.*

I could hear her running through the orchard, calling my name. It was only a matter of time.

I heard it then plain as day just over my left shoulder, a second voice. I knew it in an instant. It was Auntie Matilda. Auntie Matilda, the non-musical sister, who loved to sing but was totally tone-deaf. She used to wait until we were alone so no one else would hear and make fun of her, then she'd sing softly to me: *Don't sit under the apple tree with anyone else but me.*

That's what I was listening to. That song? Why that song? Duh — apple trees. But what about apple trees? I looked around: *Anyone else but me. Anyone else but me.* No. No. No.

I saw it then, an enormous old tree that dwarfed every other tree in the orchard. It was behind the quaint little gazebo Auntie Matilda had built, the one with the climbing roses and trellised morning glories winding around its criss-crossed slatted walls.

Don't sit under the apple tree with anyone else but me...

In my mind, she showed me a cavity inside the tree big enough to hide a person. I hopped and crutched my way over to it. My strength was giving out fast.

"Tildy?" Grace's voice was melodic, sing-song, even pleasant. That's what scared me the most. "I know you're here, honey. Come out. Come out wherever you are."

Fear squirted adrenaline into my limbs and I kept on going, around the tree to the back side, and sure enough, there it was: a narrow opening that widened into a hollow inside the tree.

I glanced around Matilda's place, a place of solitude and introspection —

Grace's voice came again, closer this time. "Try to understand, sweetie. It's nothing personal. I really love you."

— and a helluva good place to lie in wait for the nasty bitch trying to knock me off. I squeezed in through the narrow opening.

It was damp. And cold. There were icky things. Don't ask. I didn't even want to guess what they were. They poked me. And slimed me. And crawled on me. I didn't dare open my eyes. It wouldn't have done any good anyway, I couldn't see so much as my hand in front of my face.

A sense of awesome calm overcame me then, and as everything else faded into the background, I saw in my mind's eye Matilda's Heart. It was a big round shape carved into the hollow with the word *Matilda*, a plus sign, and the word *Jack*. And it was here somewhere, right in front me. I reached out and touched it. And because I found Matilda's Heart, I found Houston's grave.

Simon's words echoed in my mind: *What you seek lies thirty paces south of Matilda's heart.*

A sob caught in my throat. After all this, to finally be able to give my friend his peace.

In my mind, I called him: *Houston, Houston. I found it. I found you. Your grave. It's right here. It's over, sweetie. You can pass.*

Houston: *And so can you, sweetie, if you don't pay attention to what's going on here. She's right in front of you.*

I held my breath. Without seeing her, I sensed her, and heard her voice right outside my hiding place.

"You know. I don't feel so bad about killing you now, Tildy. If you really were my best friend, you wouldn't have sprayed me with that goddamned Mace. You would've known how hard this is for me and tried to make things easier."

Sure. You want easy?

I got easy.

I raised my shovel, stepped out behind her and —

BAM !

I dropped her with one swing of my trusty shovel.

I stared down at her crumpled form. "I can't believe I was going to leave you my dog, you bitch."

Houston appeared beside me, a wavering mist, a shadow of his former self. He gave me two thumbs up as he looked down at Grace — or Sasha — or whoever. "All right," he said. "I can dig it."

"What was that?" We both whirled at the sound of something big crashing through the orchard.

I turned to Houston, completely and utterly exhausted. "What are we going to do? I can't fight. I can't run. I can barely stand up."

"It's okay," he moved back expanding as he went. "I'll save you..."

My heart began to beat with hope as he grew brighter and brighter until he just went —

Poof! —

and turned into a watery cloud of smoke.

His voice was apologetic. "...Or not. Sorry, Tildy."

I braced for the worst as a bear-like form lumbered straight at me. I began to pray.

Dear God, let me find the light. Please don't let me wander around this freakin' apple orchard for a quarter of a century.

Then the clouds parted and the moon shone down on me and my friend John Yazzie.

"Tildy, are you all right?"

"Help me," I said. "She'll get away."

He grabbed me just as I was on the upswing again with the shovel, caught me off-balance and I collapsed in his arms.

"Oh, God," he moaned. "You're bleeding."

I looked up and tried to tell him to get the cuffs on the mean low-down slimy killer before she came to and jumped us again. But all I could do was babble. Somehow he seemed to get the message.

"It's okay, honey. Just be still."

Bill and three officers came charging into the clearing and took charge of Grace. Bill seemed kind of put out that John was doing such a good job of holding me.

A shaft of pure golden light shot from the heavens, and wrapped itself around Houston's shadowy form, cradling, then lifting him, higher and higher. The look on his face was one of pure joy.

He smiled down at me, "Thank you, Tildy. I'll save you a spot."

It brought tears of happiness to my eyes — that and the throbbing in my leg.

John looked over at the gazebo and blinked his eyes. "You see that? What was that?"

I smiled, "Houston. He's going home, John. We did it."

And then everything went black.

Epilogue

I spent three days in the hospital for observation of my head injury. Does that make me a head case? What do you think? All I know is, I saw double for two days.

My roommate was an eighty-three-year-old grandmother named Lucy Brinkerhoff who had broken her ankle while hiking Boynton Canyon.

The room got pretty cramped. It was small to begin with. But it got downright ridiculous when you added two beds, a few chairs, a TV, medicine cabinet — also two dozen baskets of flowers from just about everyone under the sun including Madame Simone, Ellen Johnson, and even (get this) Max Dunlap. There were the stacks of "Get Well" cards and way too many stuffed animals to count. And then came the visitors — Chloe, Joaquin, Bill (several times), Big John, Little John, Jo Margolis (in clean overalls yet) and Minnie Houston bearing doilies.

Who knew so many people cared about me? I was touched. Even Flake, James Flake dropped by — but I think he was hoping to catch me in "yet another" insurance scam. Did I mention all the news media? The F.B.I.? Oh and don't let me forget Lucy's six offspring, their spouses, her fifteen grandchildren, seven great-grandchildren, and the entire congregation of the Cottonwood Mormon church.

I don't think I slept a wink the entire time.

Chloe came to pick me up on the third day, as usual, chatty as hell.

"The entire town is stunned. This whole time our Grace was none other than Anita Pendleton, alias Sasha, ringleader of the Fighters for Liberated Peoples. Oh my God, Tildy. She was a murderer, for crying out loud. And you were almost another notch on her gun handle."

"Mm-hmm." I was kind of wrung out, and didn't really have much to say.

But Chloe did. "They took her down to Phoenix to stand trial. Plus she still has to serve her original sentence for all that stuff she pulled back in the seventies."

"How nice." I think the pain pills did a hell of a job.

"The Sheriff found the reporter's body. Smack-dab where you said it would be."

"Uh-huh"

"And they rounded up all those other guys, too. The Senator and Ted Cochran and the mob guys. I can't believe it, Tildy. You got 'em. You got 'em all. And nearly all by yourself."

"Yep."

Just as we got to the curb where Joaquin waited with his car, Chloe stopped pushing the wheelchair, squatted beside me and looked me square in the eye.

"Tildy, I know you're my boss, but I also think of you as my friend. I guess I'd do just about anything I could to help you."

I looked at her, focusing on the hoop through her nostril. "Didn't that hurt?"

"Focus, Tildy." Through the pink haze of drug-induced languor, I could see the hurt in her eyes. "Don't leave me out next time. Okay? Let me help."

"Okay." I said groggily. "But there's not gonna be a next time, Chloe. This was my first and last case."

She smiled. "Sure it is."

She got up and opened the car door. Haggis bounded out and leaped into my lap and made everything right again.

* * * * *

A couple of months after Houston crossed over, John picked up Haggis and me and our picnic basket at sunset and drove us out to Cathedral Rock. All the way I cradled an urn in my arms that held the ashes of our dear friend.

As the sky glowed iridescent pink, a light breeze carried the scent of cedar in its wake. It was perfect.

We toasted Houston's life with champagne.

I ate chocolate-covered strawberries (John declined — allergic to chocolate, poor baby) while he lamented the loss of his love. "For he being dead, with him is beauty slain."

Don't you just love a man who can quote Shakespeare — or understand it, for that matter?

Then we dusted the mountain with the ashes and sat for a while, just contemplating how lucky we'd both been to know such an interesting screwball as Houston Powers.

As much as I did for Houston, he did for me. He showed me how to believe in myself.

Yeah. I learned a lot about me — some good things and some not so good.

I learned I can be counted on to finish what I start.

I learned I'm smart and can do more things than I ever imagined — like driving down the side of a mountain, for instance.

But I also learned I'm a shitty judge of character. Gonna have to work on that one. Can you believe I still miss Grace? I really cared about her. How could she betray me so completely? It would take a while to get over it.

A soft, rhythmic sound distracted me from my self-analysis.

I turned to John. "You leave the radio on in the car?"

He looked at me, tears streaming down his face. "Huh-uh. Why?"

"You don't hear that?" It was getting louder.

He sniffed. "Hear what?"

"Drums. Like tom-toms."

"Tom-toms? Is this an Indian joke?"

"No."

That's when the chanting started and the rosy sunset was suddenly blotted out as Big John Yazzie, in full ceremonial dress buckskins, leaped out of nowhere to land directly in front of me. Now there's something you don't see every day.

"Hey, Big John." I said, surprised to see him.

Sheriff John cocked a puzzled brow. "Hey — what?"

"Not you. Him."

"Him. Who?"

What was this, an Abbott and Costello routine? Then I got it. He didn't see his dad. Oh, shit. You know what this means — right?

I put my hand on Little John's arm as Big John did a pretty mean war dance around us. "You talk to your dad lately?"

"Last week," Little John said. "Why?"

"Well, he's dancing circles around us."

His jaw dropped and he tried to see what I was looking at. "That can't be good." His pager went off. He read the number. "It's the Navajo Police Chief." I could see the panic rising in him. He yanked out his cell phone. "Oh, Tildy, what if something's happened to him?"

Big John stopped dancing and said, "Something has," then, "Good to see you again, Tildy."

"Oh my God, John. Are you dead?"

Sheriff John jumped to his feet. "Shit. Is he?"

"No," Big John seemed to know what he was talking about.

"No," I repeated. "He's not."

"What's wrong then?" Yazzie asked.

"I came to see you, Tildy," the old man began, "because I need you to find out who tried to kill me."

Wait a minute. Isn't this where I came in?

I thought about it before I answered. I honestly did. I just didn't hop right on the bandwagon this time. I rolled over the consequences in my mind. Like what it would mean to me in terms of time, in terms of energy, in terms of danger, then I said, "Okay. I'll do it — but only if you promise to keep those damned tom-toms out of my bedroom."

THE END?

About the Authors

 Gail has worked as a Glendale P.D. 911 dispatcher. To alleviate the pressure from her high-stress job, she finds escape in travel, reading, movies, and photography. She grew up in rural Northern Arizona and now lives in Peoria with her two crazy dogs, Zeke and Jake.

Sally has concurrently owned a travel agency and raised a family. She has a grown son and daughter, and two perfect young grandsons. Born and raised in Tucson, she now lives in Scottsdale with her husband, son, and Japanese Chins, Casey and Mini-Me. Family, travel, books, music, and her writing keep her sane or at least a reasonable facsimile.

Sally and Gail share a deep passion for Mexican food and a good story. They are award-winning script and novel writers. *The Ghost Wore Polyester* is their first novel.

To purchase additional copies of
The Ghost Wore Polyester

send this order form to:

Crossquarter Publishing Group
PO Box 8756
Santa Fe, NM 87504-8756

or fax to: (505) 438-4789 fax

_____ copies of *The Ghost Wore Polyester* at $13.95* each
_____ I want to know when *The Ghost Wore Buckskin* becomes
available. Put me on the mailing list.

* This price includes shipping and handling by US Media Mail
within the USA; please call for rates outside of the USA

Name _____

Address _____

City _____ State ___ Zip _____

Phone Number (in case of questions) (___) _____

How are you paying (please check one):

__ Check or money order made to *Crossquarter*

__ Credit card __ Visa __ Mastercard __ AmX

Account Number _____ Exp Date _____

Signature _____

New Mexico addresses, add 6.8 % sales tax.
Please allow 4-6 weeks for delivery.
www.crossquarter.com

The adventure continues at
www.ghostworepolyester.com